A GUIDE TO GROWING UP

In loving memory of Stella Namabega, Irene Namataka and Dear Old Grandad.

A GUIDE TO GROWING UP

Honest conversations about puberty, sex and God

Sarah Smith

Illustrated by Alex Webb-Peploe

MONARCH
BOOKS

Oxford UK, and Grand Rapids, USA

Published by Monarch Books
an imprint of
Lion Hudson IP Ltd
Wilkinson House, Jordan Hill Road,
Oxford OX2 8DR, England
Email: monarch@lionhudson.com
www.lionhudson.com/monarch

ISBN 978 0 85721 796 7
e-ISBN 978 0 85721 797 4

First edition 2017

Acknowledgments
Unless otherwise stated Scripture quotations taken from the Holy Bible, New International Version Anglicised. Copyright ©1979, 1984, 2011 Biblica, formerly International Bible Society. Used by permission of Hodder & Stoughton Ltd, an Hachette UK company. All rights reserved. "NIV" is a registered trademark of Biblica. UK trademark number 1448790.
Scriptures quotations marked "GNT" are from the Good News Bible © 1994 published by the Bible Societies/HarperCollins Publishers Ltd UK, Good News Bible © American Bible Society 1966, 1971, 1976, 1992. Used with permission.
Scripture quotations marked "CEV" are from the Contemporary English Version New Testament © 1991, 1992, 1995 by American Bible Society, Used with permission.
Scripture quotations marked "The Message" are taken from The Message. Copyright © by Eugene H. Peterson 1993, 1994, 1995, 1996, 2000, 2001, 2002. Used by permission of NavPress Publishing Group.

A catalogue record for this book is available from the British Library

Printed and bound in the UK, May 2017, LH29

CONTENTS

PART 4: OUR BODIES ARE PRECIOUS

PART 5: HONOURING OTHERS AND HONOURING GOD

PART 6: NEW LIFE

PART 7: HANDLE WITH CARE

FOREWORD

I wonder why you've picked up this book…

… possibly it's because, like me, you are keenly aware that not every message or role model in wider society about growing up is either good or helpful for our children. Youth culture has an uncanny knack of pedalling misinformation and double standards about self-worth and sex to young people. As those who seek to be a loving authority in our children's lives, helping them spot the lies and choose freedom, even when it's ridiculously tough to do, is essential.

Which is why I'm always on the look out for great stuff to share with my daughter and nephews (or strategically leave lying around in the hope that their curiosity might get the better of them!) to help them feel in control of their lives as they navigate the opportunities and challenges of growing up.

And whether we feel ready for it or not, conversations about sex will feature. And that's a good thing!

But even though talking with teens about sex is my day job, I find that when it comes to my own family, I tend to feel anxious about how I "should" respond to their questions – and I know I'm not alone! It seems that few topics spike as much interest and as much dread in the hearts of parents the world over. I regularly meet parents, grandparents, carers, pastors and youth workers who feel under immense pressure to "get it right", and to have all the answers when they're not even sure they know them themselves.

So you've picked up this book. I guess you want to know if it'll be any good?

I think that Sarah would be the first person to say that no book or resource ever beats an honest conversation between a loving parent and a child who feels safe enough to ask their questions about the big stuff of growing up. But if you're looking for a book that combines Biblical wisdom and accurate information about everything to do with sex (and I mean everything) with a focus on inspiring self-appreciation and responsibility, then this book is for you.

Sarah knows how to speak with young people about relationships and sex. She does it in a respectful, clear, and helpful way. She leaves them space to explore the benefits of values and boundaries, and empowers them to think for themselves and come to their own conclusions about how they will demonstrate respect, care, authenticity, and faithfulness in all their relationships.

But the great thing about this book is that it isn't a knee jerk reaction to all the unhelpful messages around growing up in our culture. This book is profoundly positive; about sex, about self, about faith, about relationships, love, boundaries, pleasure, choices – about all the sorts of things that could possibly matter when it comes to preparing our children with the richest vision for their sexuality and relationships.

Which is why I think this book will be a brilliant contribution to any young person's journey of becoming even more of the incredible human being God has created them to be.

Rachel Gardner
Founder of the Romance Academy and President of the Girls' Brigade England and Wales.

A NOTE TO PARENTS/CARERS

Dear Parent/Carer,

Cast your mind back to when you were embarking on your teenage years. Did you have any sex education at all? If so, was it any good? Did your parents/carers have conversations with you about what to expect during puberty and what sex is all about?

What are your hopes for your children in terms of how they learn about relationships and intimacy, and how their values and attitudes about sex develop?

Young people today are receiving plenty of messages about relationships and sex from the media and from society, many of which you may not feel comfortable with. The problem is, we sometimes find the topic of sex taboo and end up feeling awkward about discussing it, or simply avoid it altogether. I am really keen that we topple this taboo and create spaces to have ongoing conversations with our children that will support them in managing the changes they will go through during puberty and help them to have a healthy, positive, and realistic understanding of sex.

I hope that this book provides you with a starting point to have some of those conversations. You may wish to give it to your child to read themselves, or you may want to go through sections of it with them as and when you feel it's appropriate. Either way, I'd encourage you to have a read through it first. I have written the book prayerfully based on my understanding of what the Bible says, my knowledge as a relationships and sexual health educator, and my ten years of experience working with young people in this area. I realize that you may have different points of view to those I've raised, so do share your thoughts and opinions with your child about what I have said.

Happy reading!

Love
Sarah

FROM ME TO YOU

Dear Reader,

When I started going through puberty my mind was full of questions:

WHEN WILL I START MY PERIOD?

WHY ARE MY FRIENDS DEVELOPING BREASTS FASTER THAN ME?

CAN ANYONE NOTICE THE SMELL COMING FROM MY ARMPITS?

WHY HAVE I GOT SO MANY SPOTS?

WILL THE BOYS I FANCY EVER NOTICE ME?

WHY ARE MY ARMS AND LEGS SO HAIRY?

IS IT OK TO MASTURBATE?

WHAT IS SEX ALL ABOUT?

And as a child growing up in a Christian family, I did sometimes wonder what God thought about it all and, in particular, what he thought about sex.

So, as an adult, I decided to write the sort of book I would have liked to have read when I was going through puberty. This is that book!

I hope this book helps you to:

- improve your knowledge about your body and what happens to it during puberty;

- understand why you may experience certain emotions and feelings as you go through puberty;

- explore these topics from God's point of view. After all, bodies, puberty, relationships, and sex were all his idea!
- learn how to handle messages, images, and situations that may come your way that don't reflect God's design for bodies, relationships, and sex.

This book doesn't contain all the answers, but it is certainly going to try to help. The conversations and quotes included in the book are all from real young people (although their names have been changed). You might agree or disagree with the things they say, but I hope you find it useful to hear different perspectives.

If you have any questions along the way, do ask your parents/carers or other adult you feel comfortable with. Remember that, like me, they have been through puberty and managed to survive it!

Love
Sarah

INTRODUCTION

God loves conversation.

He especially loves conversation with you.

Any time you want to talk to God, he is always available, ready to listen and respond. God already knows what's happening, but he prefers to hear it directly from you because he has designed you to be able to interact and connect with him – to have a relationship with him.

God has also designed you to be able to have relationships with others – family, friends, school mates, all sorts of people.

It would be boring to be by ourselves all the time, wouldn't it?

We all have the ability to be kind and love others, as well as a desire to be loved and accepted.

You can show love to others in many different ways – for example, by spending time with them, helping them practically, encouraging them, being loyal, showing them affection by giving them a big hug, giving or making them gifts that you've really thought about, and letting them know they're valuable through your words and actions.

HOW WOULD YOU DEFINE LOVE?

"A strong bond between two people that is created by trust and caring for one another."

Tyrone, 15

"A feeling that you care about someone else's well-being so much that you would sacrifice things that you want for them."

Anita, 18

"The feeling of happiness between two people that makes them feel special together."

Dermot, 12

"It's about what you give, not what you get."

Emma, 13

"An emotion. It is the most powerful emotion."

Karen, 13

Human relationships were part of God's plan from the beginning. As soon as God had created Adam, the first man, he knew that something was missing. He said, "It is not good for the man to be alone. I will make a helper suitable for him" (Genesis 2:18 NIV).

So God created Eve from Adam to be his special companion, his wife. The word "helper" might give people the idea that Eve was created to help Adam with things like cleaning and making dinner. But that's not what God was talking about at all!

In this verse, the word "helper" has been translated from the Hebrew word *ezer*, a word the Bible mainly uses when talking about God. It describes something truly awesome. So this shows us that God designed Eve as a companion who would be able to provide Adam with great strength, support, and love in a way that seeks to reflect the strength, support, and love that God gives us.

It's not just about wives providing these things to their husbands. In later parts of the Bible (see Ephesians 5:22–33), we see that husbands are also to provide this strength, support, and love to their wives. Both of them are to put the other person first, which means that both are being loved and cared for. This is something that needs to be worked at, but if both partners commit to giving it their all, then marriage has the potential to be brilliant.

Putting other people first is a model for all of us in our relationships, whether we are single or married.

Being married and being single are both good things. One's not better than the other.

There are some differences between marriage and other relationships, though, and one of them is that marriage between a man and a woman is the relationship which God created sex for.

> *Then the Lord God made a woman from the rib he had taken out of the man, and he brought her to the man. The man said, "This is now bone of my bones and flesh of my flesh; she shall be called 'woman', for she was taken out of man." That is why* **a man leaves his father and mother and is united to his wife, and they become one flesh.**
>
> *Genesis 2:22–24 (NIV)*

SEX IS ONE OF GOD'S MOST BRILLIANT IDEAS!

Some people have the idea that Christianity is anti-sex, but that's not true at all – God invented sex!

Sex has the potential to be wonderful because of the way God made our bodies, hearts, and spirits – with the ability to connect to another person really deeply.

The Bible describes the husband and wife relationship as becoming "one flesh" (Genesis 2:24), but it's not just about the husband's and wife's bodies fitting together as one. It also involves both of them sharing all that they are with the other person, including their emotions and their innermost beings (their spirits). This is a big deal, so no wonder God chose for sex to be expressed in the context of a secure, committed, loving marriage.

Sex not only gives a husband and wife the opportunity to explore each other's bodies in a way that can bring them both great pleasure and joy; it also potentially gives the man's sperm a chance to reach an egg inside the woman and for the process of reproduction to start.

SO WHAT'S ALL THIS GOT TO DO WITH PUBERTY?

Well, puberty is your body's way of preparing for the future possibility of marriage, sex, and having babies (in case those are things you'd like to have). It's the time during which your body is transformed into an adult's body.

MIXED-UP SEX MESSAGES

If you watched all the music videos and studied all the lyrics from the current charts, what messages do you think they'd be giving you about relationships and sex? Do you think they would match up with God's plan for sex?

Some might, but a lot probably wouldn't.

There are many brilliant things about the media, internet, and the world around us, but on the flip side, they often give us information about sex that is unrealistic, inaccurate, and incomplete.

For example:

- Many people are watching pornography. Porn encourages people to see others as sex objects rather than precious human beings and reduces sex to something less special than it actually is.

- Marriage is often viewed as being unimportant.

- Sex is sometimes used by some people to use and abuse others.

In this book, as well as finding out more about our bodies and what happens during puberty, we'll also be finding out more about God's plan for sex.

PART I

YOUR BODY IS AMAZING

CHAPTER 1

THE AMAZING YOU

I don't know about you, but it seems to me that a lot of media focuses way too much on people's looks and body shapes. The internet, social media, TV, films, magazines, adverts, and music videos can fill our minds with an image of what a "perfect" body supposedly looks like and this can make us feel rubbish about our own bodies.

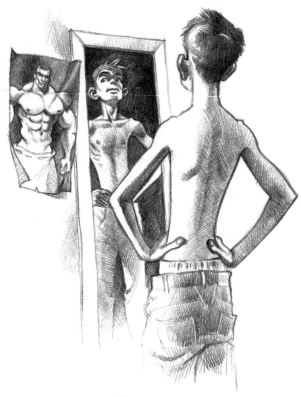

"Being insecure with your body is a huge thing because the world portrays a beautiful girl as impossible: big chest, small waist, and big bum."

Abigail, 14

"There's pressure on boys to look a certain way because they see stuff on the media and then want to have a great body."

Ethan, 14

It's so important to recognize that "perfect" images are not reality. Make-up is applied (on both women and men) and computer software is used to airbrush and filter photos, changing the way a person looks by adjusting their body shape, covering over any spots or scars, and hiding any hairs that are out of place.

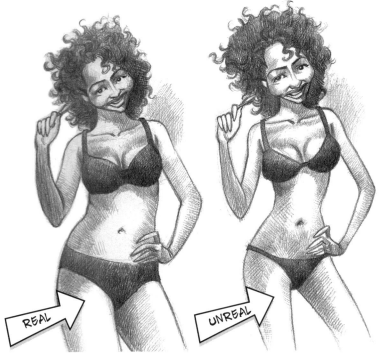

REAL

UNREAL

You'd probably be very surprised if you saw a celebrity in real life without their hair styled or without their make-up on – they're just normal human beings like the rest of us!

Rather than allowing the media to influence what you think about your body in a negative way, make yourself more aware of how amazing your body is.

Some of us have bodies that, for a number of reasons, might not function as fully as others, but they are still capable of so much. It's helpful for us to focus on what our bodies can do, rather than what they might not be able to do.

Have a think right now of all the things your body is capable of.

POWER AND WONDER

In the Bible there is a collection of songs and prayers to God called the Psalms. David (who defeated Goliath) wrote a lot of these, and in Psalm 139:14 (NIV) he writes, "I praise you because I am fearfully and wonderfully made."

"Fearfully" might sound like a strange choice of word, because we normally think of fear as being something negative. However, David chose the word to describe the *power* God uses in creating humans. Yes, we were made by our parents, but God is the designer of the whole process. He has an immense amount of power – if we could see it all we would be scared because it's so overwhelming. God is love, but his power and greatness show us that he deserves our complete respect.

So you've been made in a wonderful way that involves God's extraordinary power.

> *"For I know the plans I have for you," declares the Lord, "plans to prosper you and not to harm you, plans to give you hope and a future."*
> *Jeremiah 29:11 (NIV)*

YOUR INNERMOST BEING

Being fearfully and wonderfully made isn't just about your body; it's also about who you are as a person. Your spirit, or innermost being, is the essence of who you are. It holds your personality, your character, your values, your passions, and your dreams.

God gave each of us different gifts and abilities. We're not all good at the same things and that's absolutely fine, as God loves it when we work together, benefitting from the skills each person has. It can take time to figure out what our gifts and abilities are, so don't worry if you're not sure about yours yet. It will become clearer as you get older, but rest assured that they are there inside of you.

WHAT DOES BEING "FEARFULLY AND WONDERFULLY" MADE MEAN TO YOU?

"This makes me feel and know that I am special in God's eyes. Also, it makes me feel comfortable with myself."
Karen, 13

"I think that God says that we are made for a purpose and you have a reason to be standing on the earth."
Carlos, 11

"God designed us completely out of love and loves us just for existing."
Chloe, 14

"God has made us all different. And in his eyes we are all wonderful."
David, 12

WE'RE NOT OBJECTS

Our bodies deserve our respect. Sometimes people forget that and end up doing things like taking nude photos of themselves and sending them to other people (perhaps because someone has put pressure on them). This can have lots of negative consequences, which we'll talk about later, but basically this type of activity turns people's bodies into objects to be judged by others rather than be valued for what they actually are – amazing creations designed by God, housing our innermost beings.

HOW YOU FEEL ABOUT YOURSELF

Nobody's perfect and we all mess up from time to time, but never forget that God loves you SO much. God can even turn your mistakes into things that can help you to grow in character. You might not always feel very lovable but God loves you unconditionally, no matter what.

PAUSE AND PRAY

Let's take a little break here to have some time to chat to God.
    If you like, you might want to:

- thank God for the way he made you;

- ask God to help you see all the good things about your body and, over time, the gifts and abilities he's placed inside you;

- ask God to show you his plans for your life at the right time and help you to keep growing in character in the meantime.

We're now going to take a look at the differences between girls' and boys' bodies, particularly the sex organs involved in reproduction. They are fearfully and wonderfully made.

CHAPTER 2

BOYS ARE WONDERFULLY MADE

First, let's take a look at the male sex organs (also called male genitals).

HANGING OUT ON THE OUTSIDE

THE PENIS

Just as humans come in different shades, shapes, and sizes, the penis also comes in different shades, shapes, and sizes. There's no "right" size: all boys are different and that's normal.

One way that penises vary is that they can be circumcised or non-circumcised.

Boys are born with a fold of skin, known as the foreskin, covering the head of the penis (the glans). Circumcision is the removal of the foreskin, and this may be done for a variety of reasons.

Some parents decide to have their sons circumcised because of religious beliefs or health reasons. Some men might decide to get circumcised later in life for their own reasons. But many men are happy to remain uncircumcised.

Can you see the difference between the two?

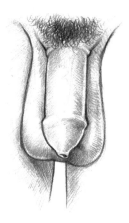
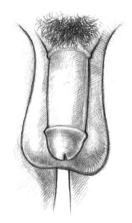

The penis is very sensitive to touch because it contains lots of nerve endings. That's why a male can experience sensations that feel good if the penis is touched or rubbed.

THE SCROTUM

The scrotum is a protective sac of skin that hangs outside of the body behind the penis, carefully holding and supporting the two testicles.

THE TESTICLES

It is in the testicles that the male sex hormone, testosterone, is made and sperm are produced. Sperm are male sex cells that can combine with a female sex cell (egg) to form the first cell of a new baby.

The testicles are very sensitive to temperature. The best temperature for sperm production is just below body temperature. That's why the testicles are held outside of a male's body, in the scrotum. The scrotum responds very quickly if the temperature is too warm or too cold. When the testicles need to cool down because it's too warm, the scrotum moves away from the body. The opposite happens if it's cold – the scrotum moves closer to the body (making it look more wrinkled) to benefit from the warmth of the body. This movement is a very clever way of controlling the temperature of the testicles.

Many boys have one testicle that is larger than the other, and one testicle may hang down lower than the other.

WHAT DOES THE BIBLE SAY ABOUT CIRCUMCISION?

Circumcision was very important to the Israelites in Old Testament times. Boys were circumcised when they were eight days old as a sign that they belonged to God.

However, the New Testament teaches us that circumcision is no longer necessary in order for boys or men to be recognized as God's people. All we need to do now to be part of God's family is to believe in Jesus, ask for forgiveness for our sins, and choose to follow the way that Jesus lived, loving and respecting everybody.

As it says in Galatians 5:6, *"For in Christ Jesus neither circumcision nor uncircumcision has any value. The only thing that counts is faith expressing itself through love"* (NIV). So God doesn't mind whether a boy is circumcised or not.

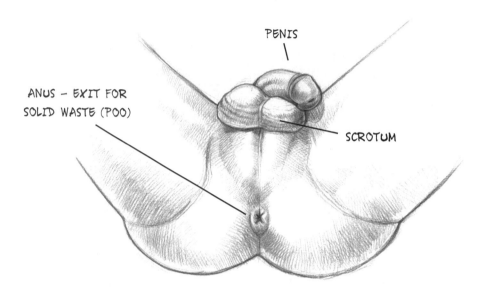

PENIS

ANUS – EXIT FOR
SOLID WASTE (POO)

SCROTUM

THE NETWORK INSIDE

EPIDIDYMIS AND SPERM DUCTS

Sperm is able to travel from the testicles to the penis through a network of different tubes. First, it travels through the epididymis and then through the sperm ducts.

THE PROSTATE GLAND AND SEMINAL VESICLES

The sperm then need an energy boost and some help to move effectively, so they mix with special fluids from the prostate gland and seminal vesicles to become semen.

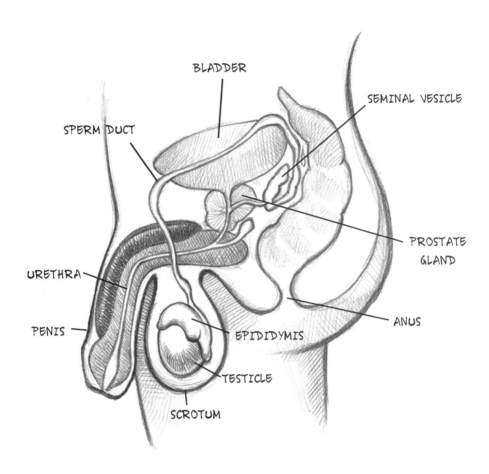

THE URETHRA

The semen then travels through the urethra (a thin tube inside the penis), until it comes out of the penis at the opening of the urethra.

Urine also travels out of the body through the urethra, but its starting point is the bladder.

CHAPTER 3

GIRLS ARE WONDERFULLY MADE

Now let's take a look at the female sex organs (also called female genitals). Some of these body parts are on the outside of the body, and some are inside.

WHAT'S ON THE OUTSIDE?

THE VULVA

The vulva is the area between a girl's legs that includes the labia, the clitoris, and the vaginal and urinary openings.

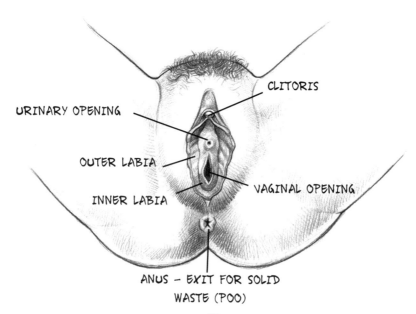

URINARY OPENING

CLITORIS

OUTER LABIA

VAGINAL OPENING

INNER LABIA

ANUS – EXIT FOR SOLID
WASTE (POO)

THE LABIA

There are two pairs of folds of skin that protect the clitoris and the vaginal and urinary openings – the outer labia and the inner labia. As with all our body parts, each girl's labia are different. The inner labia in particular vary greatly from girl to girl. Some are long and hang down, some are wide, some are narrow, some are large, some are small, most are asymmetrical (the left side looking different to the right side), some are fleshy looking, some are wrinkly looking, some have a frilly looking edge and some have a smooth edge, and they come in all different shades – some light, some dark. We're all different and that's totally normal.

THE CLITORIS

The clitoris is very sensitive to touch. It might just look like a small bump, but it is full of nerve endings, which means that when touched or caressed, pleasurable feelings and sensations flow through the female's body. In fact, when God designed the clitoris, he didn't give it any other function except to activate feelings of pleasure in the female's body.

VAGINAL OPENING

All you can see of the vagina from outside a girl's body is the opening. This

> ### FGM – NOT PART OF GOD'S DESIGN
>
> In a few cultures around the world, there is a practice of removing or altering some parts of a girl's vulva for non-medical reasons as part of their culture's tradition. In the UK this practice is called FGM (female genital mutilation) and it is illegal. It can lead to serious health implications, cause pain, and take away the possibility of feeling pleasure during sex. God designed this part of a female's body to experience pleasure, so FGM is something that goes against God's design.

looks like a small hole. For some girls it is easy to see, and for some it is quite hidden behind the labia; either way, it's normal. The vaginal opening is where menstrual blood comes out of a girl's body during her period, it's where a penis enters the female body during sex, and it's the exit for a baby when it's being born.

The hymen, a very thin layer of skin, can partially cover the vaginal opening at birth. It can stretch or break as a girl grows, through tampon use, through physical activities or the first time she has sex.

The urinary opening and the anus are close to the external female sex organs.

THE URINARY OPENING

Some people think that urine comes out of a girl's vagina, but in actual fact urine travels through and out of a separate tube – the urethra. The urethra is a short tube attached to the bladder and its opening (which is very small and just above the vaginal opening) is known as the urinary opening.

So a girl has three different openings between her legs.

WHAT'S ON THE INSIDE?

THE VAGINA

Unlike the penis, which is very obvious because it hangs outside a boy's body, the vagina is inside a girl. It is a muscular tube that connects to the uterus. It is able to expand so an erect penis can fit inside during sex and to enable a baby to pass through it during birth.

THE CERVIX

The cervix is above the vagina and it acts as a gateway between the vagina and uterus. Mucus in the cervix can change in consistency. When it is thin, it is easier for sperm to get through and when it is thick, it is more difficult for them. In a pregnant woman, the cervix closes to help keep the baby protected. When the time comes for the baby to be born, the cervix opens up again and stretches out so that the baby can make its way out of the mother's body.

THE UTERUS

The uterus (womb) is where a developing baby grows before being born. It is made up of lots of powerful muscles which expand as the baby grows and help the mother to push the baby out when the time is right.

THE FALLOPIAN TUBES

The Fallopian tubes branch out from the top of the uterus towards the ovaries. They have what look like little hands at the end of them with lots of

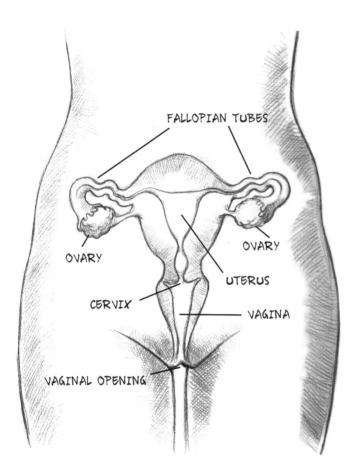

fingers. These surround the ovaries and wait for an egg (female sex cell) to be released so that they can help to direct it into the tube where it then travels towards the uterus.

THE OVARIES

There are two ovaries and these are where eggs (female sex cells) are stored. They also produce hormones, including the female sex hormones oestrogen and progesterone.

PART 2

TIME TO CHANGE

CHAPTER 4

PUBERTY: THE JOURNEY FROM CHILDHOOD TO ADULTHOOD

A journey that we all take in life is the journey from childhood to adulthood. It's on this journey that children go through puberty. For some children it starts quite early, around eight or nine years old. For others it can start much later. Whether it begins earlier or later, it's all normal. We're all different and start puberty at different times.

HORMONES - SENDING OUT INSTRUCTIONS FOR CHANGE

Why do all these changes start to happen? Well, they are caused by chemical substances called hormones, which flow through our bloodstream to different parts of the body, delivering instructions for change.

At the start of puberty, the brain releases an important kick-starter hormone that gets things going. This hormone triggers the release of other hormones that cause changes to the body such as growth and weight increase, changes to body shape, new hair growing in different places, skin and hair becoming oilier, the body becoming sweatier, and lots of new activity in the testicles for boys and in the ovaries for girls.

IT'S NOT JUST ABOUT OUR BODY

Puberty is also a time of changing emotions. You might find you have mood swings – feeling brilliant and happy one moment, and really fed up, sad, embarrassed, angry, or stressed out the next. Although these emotions might feel weird, it's important to realize they are very normal and have a lot to do with hormone activity in your brain.

HAVE YOUR EMOTIONS BEEN AFFECTED BY PUBERTY?

"Yes, I have experienced this and I don't like it because it makes you feel bad when you realize how you've been acting."

Dermot, 12

"I might start crying for a small thing and the next day, I look back and say, 'why was I crying over that?!'"

Emma, 13

"It doesn't really happen to me, but if it did I would be really careful about what I say and do."

Lily, 12

"Sometimes I feel very angry about everything."

David, 12

"I have lots of emotions. I feel uncontrollable one minute, hyper the next, and then I'm being antisocial."

Chloe, 14

"It feels like you know you are being grumpy, but you can't change how you feel."

Rohan, 14

TOP TIPS FOR DEALING WITH DIFFICULT EMOTIONS

You might find it helpful to come up with a plan to help you manage your emotions when they feel a bit challenging; for example, taking some deep breaths, finding some space to cry if you feel like it, or listening to some music that helps you to feel calm. Here are some other ideas:

"For a year or two I had a very hot temper with my family. It was a very frustrating time and I cried a lot. Now, I still get hot tempered around my period, but I just have to restrain myself from lashing out and saying something mean or hurtful."

Anita, 18

"Don't worry, it's natural, but remember to be careful about how you act if you are angry as it can have consequences."

Archie, 15

"Count to ten if you're angry."

Chloe, 14

"Maybe think about how it affects others so you can try to control it more."

Emma, 13

"Be confident in yourself no matter how rubbish you feel at times. Remind yourself that God loves you no matter what you're feeling."

Ethan, 14

The rollercoaster of emotions you might experience tends to calm down as puberty comes to an end. If you are concerned about the feelings you're having, then talk to an adult you trust. They may have experienced something similar when they were going through puberty.

BRAIN POWER

Did you know that different areas of your brain have different responsibilities and develop in different ways? The front of your brain is where important thought processes take place such as making decisions, planning, and being self-controlled. It's also the area which helps you to put yourself in another person's shoes, see their perspective, and be considerate.

This area develops over time during puberty, helping you to become more mature. While it's still developing it's really important to continue to be plugged into sound guidance from trusted adults in your life such as your parents/carers, other family members, teachers, or youth workers. You might sometimes feel that these adults are being a bit annoying (especially your parents/carers!), but they do have a lot of wisdom and support they can offer you so try to learn from the good and helpful things they are able to teach you. Your brain is especially adaptable at your age and is able to respond really well to wise and positive input.

CURIOSITY ABOUT SEX

On the journey from childhood to adulthood, many boys and girls start to get curious about sex. Not only are they hearing about sex through the media, internet, and people around them, but this curiosity is stirred further by the emotional and physical changes going on in their bodies.

You may start to be attracted to particular people. You may even feel your body responding when you think about someone you are attracted to. For example, a girl may feel a slight wetness in her vagina, and a boy may get an erection (his penis increasing in size and becoming stiff). This isn't a sign that they are ready to have sex; it's simply the body's response to a person's feelings.

Because God created sex for marriage, learning how to handle the sexual thoughts and feelings you may experience is important so that you don't get into a sexual relationship too early. We'll talk more about this later.

GOD, ARE YOU REALLY THERE?

You might sometimes wonder where God is when you're going through all these changes, especially if the changes are making you feel confused or worried. Remember, God is right there with you – even if it doesn't always feel like it.

God even knows exactly what it feels like to go through puberty because Jesus went through it. Yes, just like us, Jesus had hormones rushing around him during puberty causing him to have growth spurts, to get hairier, and to get sweatier and smellier! He would have experienced sexual feelings too and learned how to manage them.

So chat to God about what you're feeling and ask for his help if you need it.

CHAPTER 5

PUBERTY AND THE SKIN YOU'RE IN

Girls and boys have some big differences in their puberty journeys, but there are some similarities. A major similarity is what happens to the skin:

- Skin becomes oilier, which means that acne can develop.

- More sweat is produced, which means that the body becomes smellier.

ACNE

Did you know that acne doesn't just form in obvious places like the face? It can also appear on the chest, neck, upper back, shoulders, and in other areas.

So why does this happen? What causes acne? To find out, we need to understand what happens below the surface of our skin…

Skin contains a natural oil called sebum. It's produced in the dermis, where the oil glands are, and this oil helps to protect the skin and stop it from drying out. During puberty, when hormones are triggering lots of changes in the

body, the oil glands respond by producing more and more sebum. The skin finds it difficult to cope with this extra sebum and the pores (the tiny holes in the skin) can get blocked.

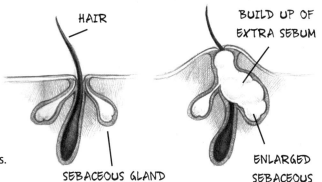

Dead skin cells and bacteria can also contribute to blocked pores. Whiteheads, blackheads, or pus-filled spots form because of the blockages.

TREATING ACNE

There are lots of treatments available from pharmacies, and, for more serious acne, doctors can recommend the right treatment.

Try not to pick at spots – this will only make it worse and may cause scarring. If you do get scars, they may fade over time, but it's much better to avoid getting scars in the first place.

Wash skin gently. Excessive washing can dry out the skin and scrubbing can aggravate the skin even more.

People often feel like hiding away, not going out, and not letting anyone see their skin when they've got acne. But remember that who you are as a person is more important than whether you have acne or not. Choose to be positive!

If you have acne, then you're in good company – a lot of people get it at some point in their lives, especially during puberty, but it does occur in adults too.

Remember that it won't last forever, treatment will help, and it's just a sign that you are developing.

"Sometimes I get spots on my face, which gets a bit embarrassing and annoying."

Emma, 13

WHAT ADVICE WOULD YOU GIVE TO PEOPLE ABOUT ACNE?

"Don't be too insecure about getting acne because loads of people get it and it's just a part of life."

Abigail, 14

"Don't worry about it. Don't be afraid and be proud."

Carlos, 11

"Try to be patient and touch your face as little as possible throughout the day to avoid irritation."

Anita, 18

"I had two bouts of acne. It was painful and so noticeable, but my doctor gave me some medicine to put on my face and after a few months it cleared. I still use the medicine."

Natalie, 19

"Don't invest your sense of self-worth in how your face looks. It's normal to have spots."

Harry, 19

MYTH BUSTERS

MYTH *Only people that don't wash properly get spots.*

TRUTH *The root cause of acne is excess sebum being produced, not a lack of washing. However, washing gently with a mild facial wash in the morning and evening will help remove dead skin cells, bacteria, and excess oil on the skin's surface and this is beneficial to the skin.*

MYTH *Spots are always caused by sweets, chocolate, and greasy food.*

TRUTH *As above, the root cause of acne is excess sebum rather than diet. However, some studies show that certain foods may impact the skin's condition and aggravate acne for some people. A doctor would be able to give advice on individual cases.*

47

SWEATINESS AND SMELLINESS

What about the interesting smells that the body starts to give off during puberty? When we get warm our body's natural response is to sweat, as this helps to cool the body down. During puberty, sweat glands in the dermis layer of the skin get very active and, just as oil glands produce more oil, sweat glands produce more sweat. Sweat itself doesn't actually have a smell, but when it stays on the skin, bacteria on the skin very quickly start to feed on it, releasing a smell which we call body odour. We all have our own body odour and this doesn't usually smell very nice to other people! So it's important to take a shower or bath every day, and take an extra one after doing sport if you can as you'll be sweaty again. Body parts that get particularly smelly are under the arms (use an anti-perspirant deodorant), the feet, and the genital area, so pay special attention to cleaning those areas. Use shower gel or a mild soap (using un-perfumed ones or those for sensitive skin can be a good idea as they are gentler).

HAVE YOU NOTICED THAT YOU SWEAT MORE SINCE STARTING PUBERTY?

"Yes, I smell more, so I use deodorant."

David, 12

"I have a shower every day. I use deodorant and sometimes a bit of perfume."

Emma, 13

"I became quite sweaty at the beginning of puberty even when I hadn't engaged in much exercise."

Rohan, 14

"Hygiene is very important – washing and keeping clean when your body starts to produce lots of smells, it's really necessary."

Natalie, 19

"I seem to be smelling a bit worse and my hair is more greasy."

Archie, 15

"Wash often everywhere, even if you think you don't need it."

Ethan, 14

CHAPTER 6

PUBERTY - THE BOY'S JOURNEY

Puberty kicks off for boys at around eleven to twelve years old, but it's normal for it to start earlier or later than this too. Generally it can start from any age between nine and fourteen years old. We're all different and there's no wrong or right time for it to start.

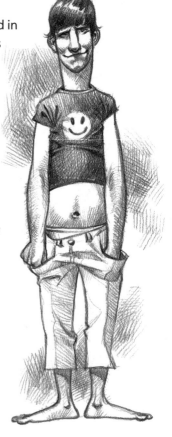

Some boys may feel like they've been left behind in the growth department because all of their mates are already much taller than they are. And other boys may feel like they really stand out because their growth spurt started early and they're now towering above their mates. But there's no need to worry. Because we start puberty at different times, there will be some differences between you and your friends. Just remember, your body will become an adult's body at exactly the right time for you.

The action of hormones throughout the body triggers all sorts of changes.

BODY SHAPE

- Arms, legs, hands, and feet experience a growth spurt first.

- The body increases in weight and height.

- Upper body gets broader.

- Muscles develop and get more defined.

- The penis and testicles increase in size.

EXPANDING IN DIFFERENT DIRECTIONS

Certain parts of the body, such as arms, legs, hands, and feet grow at a very fast rate compared with other body parts. This is all normal and the growth evens out eventually.

Some young men keep growing into their twenties, even when puberty has come to an end. It's important to remember that some people are naturally smaller than others and some people are naturally bigger, so even when our growing is complete, we all look different to each other and that's a good thing.

Something that many boys experience during the early years of puberty is a swelling under the nipples that makes it look like breasts are going to grow. If this happens to you, don't worry! It's just the result of hormone activity. It's temporary and the swelling and tenderness do go away. You can always see a doctor if you are concerned, but rest assured it is a normal part of puberty for many boys.

51

IS THE SIZE OF MY PENIS OK?

During puberty, the penis gets longer and thicker. This happens gradually over a few years.

Some boys worry that their penis is too small or is the wrong shape. This is because certain media messages suggest that, when it comes to sex, "bigger is better"; this is not true, because good sex is much more to do with the relationship between two people than the size of their body parts.

When the penis becomes erect (stiff and hard) it increases in size anyway. In actual fact, many penises that look smaller when soft can increase more in size during an erection than a penis that is larger when soft, evening out the difference.

BODY HAIR

- Pubic hair appears around the genitals.

- Armpit hair makes an appearance.

- Facial hair appears.

- Hair on the arms and legs becomes more obvious and can also appear in other places like the chest, back, bottom, the back of the hands, and on the tummy.

- Hair on the head gets oilier and needs washing more regularly.

Some boys become very hairy and others don't grow many new hairs at all. Either way it's fine and totally normal.

Some guys prefer not to have facial hair so they shave it off with an electric shaver or a razor with a blade. If using a razor with a blade you need a lubricant like shaving gel/cream to help the razor glide smoothly over the face. With an electric shaver you don't need to wet your face or use a lubricant, but it's really important to read the instructions carefully.

Chat to your dad or another male relative or older male friend to get their advice and to show you what to do when the time comes.

THE VOICE

During puberty a boy's voice changes as the voice breaks.

This happens because the voice box (the larynx) expands, causing the sound and tone of the voice to change. For a while this means a boy's voice swings from high to low as he's talking. This can feel embarrassing, but it is totally normal and will eventually even out to become a deeper tone.

BOYS, WHAT DO YOU THINK ABOUT PUBERTY?

"The best thing about growing up is getting taller because I am small."

Carlos, 11

"Some of the best things about puberty are getting taller and growing a moustache, because it makes you feel older."

Dermot, 12

"In my opinion, I quite like it that my voice broke because I used to have a high voice."

Rohan, 14

"Nothing particularly exciting happens, but looking back, it's nice to have a deeper voice and be taken more seriously. Facial hair makes you look more grown up and that's great for most things in life."

Harry, 19

"Laughing at our voice breaks is fun and getting a manly voice."

Archie, 15

GIRLS, WHAT ADVICE WOULD YOU GIVE TO A BOY IF THEY WERE FEELING INSECURE ABOUT THEIR BODY?

"Don't worry, just be natural."

Emma, 13

"In my opinion, all boys look beautiful in their own way. You will find people who love you for who you are, not what you look like."

Karen, 13

CHAPTER 7

SPECTACULAR SPERM ADVENTURES

During puberty, under the instruction of the male sex hormone, testosterone, the testicles go from being a fairly quiet place where nothing much happens to very active sperm factories producing vast quantities of sperm. In fact, the number of sperm produced can be more than 100 million a day!

Each individual sperm has a mission while it is still in the male's body: to become the best sperm it can be to increase its chances of fertilizing (being united with) a female's egg. When a sperm is first formed, it is just a small round cell, but it needs to grow and develop a tail to help it swim as fast as possible in the race to reach an egg first. So each sperm stays in the testicles for about 70 days until it is fully grown.

Even when it's fully grown, the sperm still has some work to do. It moves to the epididymis, where it matures, gaining the ability to be able to swim and fertilize an egg.

From the epididymis the sperm move through the sperm ducts, after which some fluids mix with them from the seminal vesicles and the prostate gland to produce semen. Part of the fluids gives the sperm protection and helps them to survive if they enter a female's body.

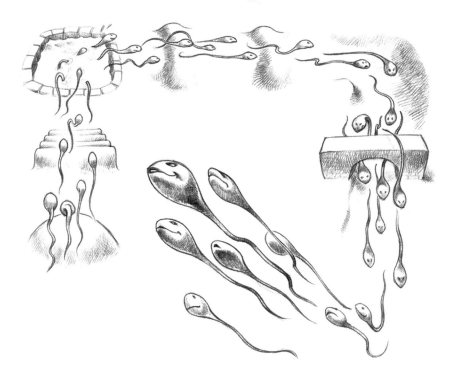

EJACULATIONS

During an ejaculation (a release of the semen out of the penis), semen travels into the urethra and it bursts out from the end of the penis. It is a white or off-white fluid.

The semen that spurts out contains millions of sperm. It can be as many as 500 million! That sounds like a huge amount, but you can't see them unless you look at the semen under a microscope.

Ejaculation occurs during sexual intercourse, but it can also occur when a male is sexually excited in other ways – even through his dreams. The release of sperm is accompanied by a rush of pleasurable feelings which is called an orgasm or climax.

WET DREAMS

During puberty it is common for boys to start having pleasurable dreams because of the increased hormonal activity in their body. These dreams can trigger an ejaculation, and when the boy wakes up he might find that his tummy and skin around the penis, his nightwear, and sheets might be sticky and wet from the semen that's been released. That's why these dreams are called "wet dreams".

The first time it happens it can feel quite strange and confusing, but it's completely normal and nothing to feel guilty about.

WHAT DO YOU THINK ABOUT WET DREAMS?

"A boy might feel good when he wakes up after a wet dream or he might feel a bit weird because he doesn't know what just happened."

David, 12

"Not having had one, I might be a bit embarrassed."

Rohan, 14

"A wet dream is when you have a dream of someone you like and finding out in the morning you've ejaculated, but it's honestly nothing to worry about. You may feel good or embarrassed, but don't worry, it's natural."

Ethan, 14

"I don't know what it feels like because I haven't experienced it."

Carlos, 11

ERECTIONS

Generally, for an ejaculation to happen, the penis has changed position and shape – this is called an erection. The penis goes from being soft and hanging down to becoming stiff, bigger, and pointing out from the body.

Why does this happen? Well, when a penis is soft, blood flows freely in and out of it, just as it flows all around the body. An erection occurs when

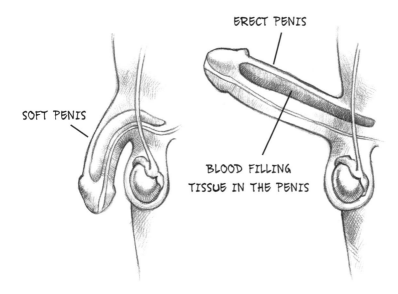

ERECT PENIS

SOFT PENIS

BLOOD FILLING
TISSUE IN THE PENIS

more blood flows into the penis and is held there, packed into its tissue, making it expand. When the blood starts flowing out again the penis returns to its normal soft state.

So what makes extra blood flow into the penis in the first place? Well, the penis is very sensitive to touch because of all the nerve endings it contains. This means that when the penis is rubbed or touched, it feels good. The body responds to these feelings of pleasure by releasing more blood into the penis.

An erection can also happen without the penis actually being touched. If a boy is thinking about someone he's attracted to or is thinking about something sexual, then his body may become sexually excited. The natural response to this feeling is for blood to fill the penis, leading to an erection.

It is very common for boys to have a few erections during the night without even being aware of it and to wake up with an erection. This isn't usually linked to what the boy is dreaming about, but is more to do with how the blood flows around the body at night. A full bladder can also trigger an erection.

Sometimes an erection happens for no obvious reason at all. This can feel embarrassing, but don't worry – it's very unlikely that anyone will notice. A good way of losing an erection is to focus on thinking about something else.

Although erections can happen from a young age, they become more common during puberty because they can be triggered by new thoughts and feelings to do with sex, which is a natural part of growing up.

Having an erection doesn't mean that ejaculation has to occur or that a boy has to have sex. Millions of sperm are being produced all the time, but they are simply absorbed by the body after a while if they are not released.

MYTH BUSTERS

MYTH *All boys have wet dreams.*

TRUTH *Many boys don't have wet dreams. Either way it's normal.*

MYTH *There is a bone inside the penis.*

TRUTH *The penis is made of different types of tissue and blood vessels, but no bones. Some people think there must be a bone inside because of how the penis looks when a male is having an erection, but erections are simply caused by blood filling the tissue of the penis.*

CHAPTER 8

PUBERTY - THE GIRL'S JOURNEY

Puberty starts earlier for girls than for boys, at around ten or eleven years old, but it's normal for it to start earlier or later than this too. Generally it can start from any age between eight and fourteen years old.

The action of hormones brings transformation to different parts of the body.

BODY SHAPE

- Arms, legs, hands, and feet all experience a growth spurt first.

- The body increases in weight and height.

- Breasts develop and grow and hips get wider.

EXPANDING IN DIFFERENT DIRECTIONS

Girls get taller and also gain weight because of the growth of bones, muscles, internal organs, and fat. A certain amount of fat is really important for the production of the female sex hormone, oestrogen, and helps the body to function well.

Many girls worry about their body shape, especially when they are gaining weight. But it's really important to realize that weight gain (as long as it's not linked to eating too much unhealthy food like crisps, chocolate, chips, burgers, etc.) is a normal and healthy process during puberty.

BREASTS

One of the first signals that puberty has begun in a girl is that the area around her nipples will feel a bit sore and breasts will start to develop. The soreness and tenderness are temporary.

Breasts grow over a period of around two to four years. It is very common for one breast to grow a bit faster than the other. By the time each breast has fully developed they will be roughly the same size, though one may still be a bit bigger than the other.

In the centre of the breast there is a nipple and a darker circular area of skin called the areola. Sometimes this area has small lumps and bumps on and around it and can also have some hairs growing from it.

Breasts vary from female to female and come in all different shades, shapes, and sizes. Inside, they contain fatty tissue and also milk glands which are there to produce milk if she has children.

Just as boys can worry that their penis is not big enough or the right shape or size, girls can have similar worries about their breasts. There is no "right" breast size – each girl's breasts are exactly the right size for her.

Some people say that bigger breasts are more beautiful, and this can make girls with small breasts feel bad and wish theirs were bigger. Some people say that small breasts are more beautiful, and this can make females with bigger breasts feel bad and wish theirs were smaller. It's good to feel comfortable with your own breast size whether small, medium, or big.

When the time comes, the right boys to be dating and the right man to marry are not those who are focused on your breasts, but those who are focused on who you are. All you need to remember is that no matter what shape, colour, or size, all breasts are beautiful!

When breasts start developing, you might feel like you'd be more comfortable wearing a bra, especially when exercising. There are lots of different bras to choose from, so you might want to ask your mum, or another female relative or friend, to help you buy your first one. Look out for a shop that does bra fittings so that they can help you find the best fit.

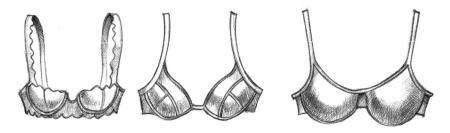

BODY HAIR

- Hair on the head gets oilier and needs washing more regularly.
- Pubic hair appears around the vulva.
- Armpit hair makes an appearance.
- Hair on the arms and legs becomes more obvious.
- Hair above the upper lip may become more noticeable for some girls.

All this new hair is completely natural and normal. Many girls don't mind it and are happy to let it grow naturally. Others prefer to remove some of it. There are a variety of hair-removal methods, so if it's something you are thinking about, then it's a good idea for you to chat to your mum or another woman you trust to get some advice, especially as some hair removal methods can irritate the skin.

   You might wonder what the point of having all this new hair is. There are several reasons, including the fact that it's simply a sign that your body is developing and becoming more sexually mature. Pubic hair has an additional important function – it provides protection for the vulva area, keeping any dirt particles out. So, it's a good thing!

VAGINAL DISCHARGE

During puberty, or just before, girls start to produce vaginal discharge. This clear, white or off-white/yellowish fluid that comes out of a girl's vagina can be quite thin and sticky or much thicker. It is totally normal and actually helps the vagina to keep healthy.

GIRLS, WHAT DO YOU THINK ABOUT PUBERTY?

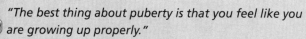

"The best thing about puberty is that you feel like you are growing up properly."

Joy, 12

"During puberty, you can relate to other girls more and have conversations with them which brings you closer."

Chloe, 14

"I used to be very concerned about having a small chest. I'd stuff my bra and be really self-conscious about them. I've since accepted them."

Natalie, 19

"Sometimes, I wish that I had more of an hourglass figure (bigger breasts and hips), but I have to remember that God made me the way I am and he never makes mistakes."

Abigail, 14

BOYS, WHAT ADVICE WOULD YOU GIVE TO GIRLS IF THEY ARE FEELING INSECURE ABOUT THEIR BODY?

"Girls should remember that you're beautiful as you are."

Tyrone, 15

"When I've been attracted to girls, it's not really been their body that I've been attracted to. I have been attracted to them as people and that has made me attracted to their bodies, not the other way round."

Harry, 19

CHAPTER 9

EXCELLENT EGG ADVENTURES

During puberty, the ovaries become a hub of activity for girls. Hormones give the egg cells that have been stored in the ovaries the opportunity to mature and leave the ovaries.

For many girls this starts to happen between the ages of around eleven and fourteen. For some, it can happen as early as eight, and for others it may

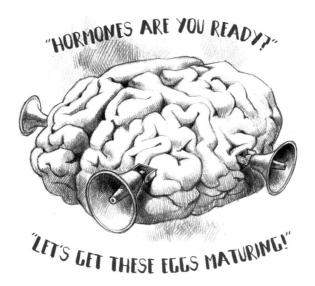

"HORMONES ARE YOU READY?"

"LET'S GET THESE EGGS MATURING!"

not happen until they are sixteen. It will happen when a girl's body is ready and that's different for each girl.

One egg cell matures each month, and when it is ready it bursts out of the ovary. This is called ovulation. This mature egg then starts travelling through the Fallopian tube towards the uterus.

In the meantime, the uterus has been preparing itself to be a safe place where a baby could develop by making its lining thicker with extra blood and tissue.

PERIODS

If the egg does not meet a sperm (meaning that a baby won't develop), this extra lining simply disintegrates and travels out of the uterus, through the cervix, and out of the vagina.

A girl doesn't see the egg coming out of her vagina because of its small size. What she does see is a bloody fluid, which is a mix of blood and tissue from the extra lining. This is called menstrual blood and is known as a period. The whole process of the bleeding starting, finishing, a new egg maturing, ovulation, and the bleeding starting again is called the menstrual cycle.

The menstrual cycle lasts for approximately twenty-eight to thirty days. This means that a girl will have a period approximately once a month. As with

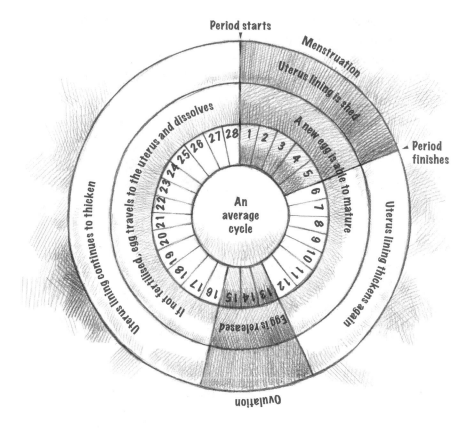

Period starts

Menstruation

Uterus lining is shed

A new egg is able to mature

Period finishes

Uterus lining thickens again

Ovulation

Egg is released

If not fertilised, egg travels to the uterus and dissolves

Uterus lining continues to thicken

An average cycle

1 2 3 4 5 6 7 8 9 10 11 12 13 14 15 16 17 18 19 20 21 22 23 24 25 26 27 28

everything else to do with our bodies, we're all different, so some girls will have a shorter cycle and for some it will be longer.

The duration of the period varies as well and tends to be between two and eight days.

A girl can use either a sanitary towel, which fits into her knickers, or a tampon, which fits inside her vagina to absorb the blood flow.

Some girls prefer sanitary towels and some girls prefer tampons. Choose whichever is most comfortable for you. If you find it difficult to insert a tampon, don't worry. You can always try using them again at a later stage if you want to.

"I use sanitary towels because I find them easier."
Lily, 12

"I use pads, but tampons for swimming and sport."
Karen, 13

"I used to be really scared about using tampons so I'd stick to towels. I didn't start using tampons until I was about 18."
Natalie, 19

When a girl starts her period, it can take a while for the body to get into a regular rhythm of periods. You can be prepared by carrying a sanitary towel or tampon with you when possible – for example, in your school bag.

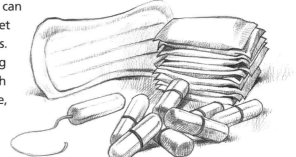

Women stop having periods around their late forties to mid-fifties. This stage is called the menopause. Because their ovaries are no longer releasing eggs, they won't be able to get pregnant. Periods may also stop temporarily before then for a number of reasons including pregnancy, illness, stress, or through doing a lot of physical exercise.

WHAT ELSE CAN HAPPEN?

The menstrual cycle really is an amazing process. However, for many girls it doesn't usually feel amazing.

A few days before a period starts, and during a period, some girls get cramp-like pains. If this occurs there are some things that can help. Holding a hot water bottle where the pain is or having a warm bath can help, as heat helps to relax the muscles. Pain relief tablets can also help. Many girls find that the pain reduces as they get older.

A girl may notice other things happening to her body in the run-up to her period. These symptoms may start even two weeks before the period. They can include:

- breast area feeling tender;

- tiredness;

- acne;

- feeling bloated;

- headaches.

As well as physical changes, a girl may feel very emotional and experience mood-swings, especially just before her period starts. These physical and emotional changes are known as PMS (pre-menstrual syndrome) or PMT (pre-menstrual tension).

There are things a girl can do to help ease the symptoms. Eating a healthy,

balanced diet can make a difference. That means eating plenty of fruit and vegetables, and cutting down on caffeine, processed foods, and foods that are very salty like crisps and chips. Too much salt stops water flowing through the body properly and that can make you feel bloated. Drinking plenty of water is also helpful, as is regular exercise and getting enough sleep.

If a girl experiences PMS very strongly, a doctor will be able to help.

WHAT'S YOUR EXPERIENCE OF PERIODS BEEN LIKE?

"I have started my period, and in my point of view, it is annoying because I get headaches and stomach cramps."
Emma, 13

"Mine aren't particularly painful, but I do get hungry."
Karen, 13

"I have experienced feeling really emotional. On my period, I always cry for stupid reasons that are no big deal. But I have to remember that it's because of my period, which is how I control myself."
Abigail, 14

"Exercise helps me when I'm on my period."
Chloe, 14

"Periods are a bit uncomfortable at first, but you get used to it."
Joy, 12

MYTH BUSTERS

MYTH *Tampons can go up too far and get lost in a girl's body.*

TRUTH *The cervix prevents tampons from going further upwards.*

MYTH *Once a girl starts her periods, she is ready to have a baby.*

TRUTH *It is possible for a girl to get pregnant once her ovaries start releasing eggs, but her reproductive system is still likely to have some developing to do to make the delivery of a baby safe. Being ready involves much more than being physically ready anyway. It takes time for a couple to be emotionally ready and to have access to the resources to be able to bring up a child.*

Do chat with your mum, another female relative or an older female friend if you want to find out more.

PAUSE AND PRAY

- What did you think about this section of the book? How has it made you feel? Sometimes people can feel embarrassed about talking about these things, but hopefully you can see that it's all part of God's design and that puberty is a good thing, even though it can be challenging.

- How do you feel about the changes going on in your body, or the changes to come? If there's anything concerning you, do chat to God about it and speak to your parents/carers or another trusted adult too.

- Are you struggling with certain emotions like anger, worry, having mood swings, feeling bad about yourself or not feeling likeable? Invite God into your heart and ask him to calm your mind and thoughts and to help you through any difficult situations you are experiencing. Some of these feelings may be related to the hormone activity that's going on in your body. Ask God to help you manage these feelings and to help you remember how much he loves you and how precious and important you are to him.

PART 3

SEXUAL FEELINGS, SEX, AND ATTRACTION

CHAPTER 10

MASTURBATION - A PERSONAL CURIOSITY

As we have seen, hormones are very busy during puberty, triggering lots of changes. With all this activity going on, it's no surprise that many boys and girls start to become more curious about their bodies.

The outer layer of our skin contains millions of nerve endings, which means that our skin is sensitive to touch.

The penis, clitoris, labia, and area around the vagina are very sensitive, because they contain a large number of these nerve endings. When this skin is touched the body may experience rushes of pleasurable feelings. This can continue into an intense sensation which is called an orgasm or climax.

During puberty (and sometimes before), boys and girls become more aware of these pleasurable feelings and some want to touch or rub these parts of their body to experience these sensations.

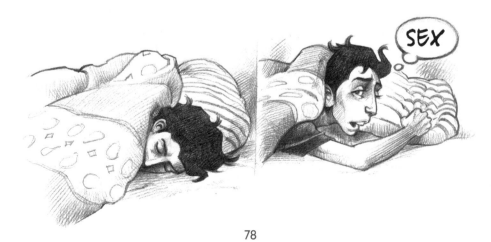

This touching or rubbing of the sexual body parts is called masturbation. Masturbation is very common and is a natural response to becoming aware of the sensations the body is capable of having. It is also absolutely normal not to masturbate.

Some people say masturbation is a bad thing to do, but others say it's fine because there is nothing medically wrong or physically harmful about doing it. So, which view is correct? Is it ok or not ok?

Does the Bible help us out with any words of wisdom about masturbation?

Well, if you look in the index of the Bible, the word "masturbation" isn't there. There are no verses that specifically talk about masturbation.

If we look more closely, though, we can find that the Bible has lots to say about things related to masturbation, which can help us.

SELF-CONTROL

In 1 Corinthians 6:12 it says, "Someone will say, 'I am allowed to do anything.' Yes; but not everything is good for you. I could say that I am allowed to do anything, but I am not going to let anything make me its slave" (GNT).

This verse says that we can make our own choices and do what we want; however, even though we can do what we want, not everything is helpful for us. In fact, we can start to get controlled by things we do and find that we can't stop doing them.

Masturbation can be like that for some people. Because it makes the body feel good, some people want to do it a lot. It's as if the body is controlling the person instead of the person controlling their body. That's why the verse says, "I'm not going to let anything make me its slave". It's saying, "I'm not going to let anything take control over me", and that includes masturbation.

If a person thinks that they are masturbating too much and that they are being controlled by the sexual feelings in their body, it's time to take the control back! The person can come up with a plan to commit to not masturbating for at least a day, a few days, a week, two weeks, a month, two months or whatever will be a good challenge for them. If they keep repeating this, extending the time period each time, they'll find that they gain control rather than being controlled by the desire to masturbate.

LUST

As well as needing to be in control of our bodies, we also need to be in control of our minds. It is totally normal to be attracted to different people as we grow up, and this can involve thinking about them a lot. But we have to be careful not to let our thoughts get out of control and become lustful.

Lust is strong sexual desire that goes beyond normal healthy physical attraction. Its driving force is self-centred, and it is more interested in getting short-term satisfaction than in giving true love and friendship that will last.

A big issue with masturbation is that, although it starts out being a natural curiosity about the body, it can become unhealthy because as we get older it is often linked with lustful thoughts about people. We can end up reducing a person we are thinking of to just a sex object rather than seeing them as a whole person. So, although masturbation is a common response to our sexual feelings, it is not necessarily healthy for the mind because of the thoughts that can be happening at the same time.

If someone simply focuses on the pleasurable feelings in their body when they masturbate, rather than thinking sexual thoughts about someone, then this is much healthier for the mind, but it's quite hard to do!

THE BIGGER PICTURE OF SEX

Even though masturbation can make the body feel good, it is an incomplete version of sex because the relationship part is missing. This can make a person feel a bit empty after doing it. It just doesn't match up to the brilliant gift of sex as God intended it to be.

God is full of love and compassion for us, and he doesn't want people to be burdened with feelings of guilt and shame when they masturbate. But perhaps he wants us to know that masturbation can cause us to be distracted from what sex is really designed for and that it can lead to bigger issues later in life if we let it control us rather than us controlling it.

MYTH BUSTERS

MYTH *People who masturbate go blind.*

TRUTH *Masturbation does not affect eyesight at all.*

MYTH *If you masturbate, hairs will grow on the palms of your hands.*

TRUTH *Just like the soles of our feet and our lips, palms are covered by a type of skin which doesn't contain hair follicles, so hair growth is not possible whether a person masturbates or not!*

CHAPTER 11

WHAT IS SEX?

Now that we've covered what happens during puberty, let's start talking about sex in more detail.

God could have come up with a way of making new human beings that was boring, just required one person, or involved following some instructions, like putting together a wardrobe or following a recipe.

But God came up with something way more interesting than that!

He gave man and woman the opportunity to experience a special relationship with each other. It would involve them committing to each other, being really good friends, and loving each other like no other person. It would be different to friendships with other people because it would connect them in a deeper way physically, emotionally, and spiritually.

This special relationship is called "marriage".

Sex was designed to be an important part of marriage, but what exactly is sex? Well, the physical side of sex involves all sorts of touch – hugging, kissing, and caressing each other's bodies. Each of these things individually is not "having sex", but they can play a part in the build-up to sexual intercourse.

During sexual intercourse (and here we are talking about the type of sex where babies can be created), the man's erect penis enters the woman's vagina. God designed the man's and woman's bodies to fit so they could experience complete closeness with each other. Their bodies move together in a way that can potentially bring great pleasure to both of them. The pleasurable feelings they experience can continue into an intense sensation which is called an orgasm or climax.

New life can be created through sex, but as we can see, the possibility of making babies is just a part of what sex is about. God designed it to feel good and to connect a wife and husband in a really intimate way.

It's not just about bodies though. During sex and just after, certain chemicals are released in the brains of both partners. The release of these chemicals tends to lead to a deeper sense of emotional and spiritual attachment between the couple. It really is an amazing process.

Many people choose to have sex without making a commitment to the other person, but why do you think that God intended sex to be shared within the commitment of marriage? Well, here are some possible reasons:

- Sex needs to be handled with care. Placing it within the secure and safe boundaries of a loving, faithful, and respectful marriage (which is God's dream for all marriages) means that the emotional and spiritual connection that deepens through having sex can be treasured and developed over time.

- God asks us to be holy – to be set apart from the rest of the world. Getting married gives a couple the opportunity to publicly declare their lasting commitment to each other and to make it clear that they are setting themselves apart as a new unit.

- Sex connects two people together. If this connection is broken by the two people not being in a relationship any more, it can be very painful for one or both of the people. If a married couple both pay special attention to the promises that they made during their wedding ceremony, this connection can be protected.

- A good marriage helps to provide a loving and stable environment in which a child can grow and flourish.

WHAT ARE YOUR VIEWS ON SEX?

"God designed sex as a gift for married couples to celebrate their marriage."

Abigail, 14

"... Otherwise it will lose its meaning. It should be something special."

Rohan, 14

"God wanted sex to be within marriage to stop sex becoming senseless."

Harry, 19

"It's something special and it means that there is something only you and your partner have shared."

Karen, 13

"It is a really personal, special, and intimate act."

Natalie, 19

"If you wait until marriage I think the intimacy is higher."

Tyrone, 15

DIFFERENT TYPES OF SEX

The type of sex we have been talking about here is vaginal penetrative sex – where a man inserts his penis into a woman's vagina. Women can get pregnant through vaginal penetrative sex.

Oral sex is where a person uses their tongue and mouth to caress another person's genitals.

Anal sex is where a man inserts his penis into another person's anus.

Pregnancy can't occur through oral or anal sex, but STIs (sexually transmitted infections) can be transmitted through both oral and anal sex (as well as vaginal penetrative sex) if either person is already infected.

Anal sex carries more health risks than other types of sexual activity because:

- The lining of the anus is very delicate and can easily be damaged which can increase the chance of infections being spread.

- The anus doesn't produce natural wetness (lubrication) in the same way the vagina does, to help the penis move inside it. This increases the risk of the lining getting damaged.

- The key job of the anus is to be an exit for solid waste (poo) out of the body. This means that anal sex could bring the penis into contact with traces of bacteria around the anus and this can cause health issues.

So, although some couples choose to have anal sex, it can have some serious health risks. Careful consideration needs to be taken as to whether both people are really comfortable with it (a lot of people aren't) and the risks involved. After all, the anus is a very important part of the body.

MYTH BUSTERS

MYTH *Sex is always amazing.*

TRUTH *Sex doesn't always feel good. It can be a bit awkward or uncomfortable or not go quite as planned. It's important that the couple are able to talk openly and honestly to each other, so they're able to learn about each other's bodies over time and understand what feels good for both of them.*

MYTH *It's a good idea to have sex before you get married so that you know what to do.*

TRUTH *There's not a set way of having sex because different people enjoy different types of touch. So having sex with other people first won't necessarily help a person to have good sex with their future wife or husband. In fact, it might make it more difficult because when they get married they may compare their wife or husband to the people they've already had sex with. They might also still feel a connection to those people which can be really unhelpful.*

CHAPTER 12

BODIES AND SEX ON SCREEN

So much of how bodies and sex are represented by the media and on the internet is the opposite of God's masterplan for sex. A lot of the potential beauty and wonder of sex is being stripped away by society. It's often portrayed and experienced in a casual and diluted way, rather than being highly valued and recognized as the precious and loving expression of togetherness it was designed to be.

Pornography (porn) in particular has become a growing problem.

PORNOGRAPHY

Pornography is any video clip, film, image, or writing that shows or talks about sexual acts or sexual organs in a way that is designed to excite people sexually.

Can you think of any reasons why porn doesn't fit God's model for relationships and sex? Here are some:

- Porn focuses on the physical side of sex (usually in an unrealistic way) rather than what it means to have a real relationship. This means that it is showing a very incomplete version of sex.

- Porn presents people as sex objects and encourages people who are watching to lust after them.

- Some people in porn have been forced into it, and don't actually want to be involved.

- Porn actors/actresses are often chosen because they look a certain way and many have had all their pubic hair removed – it's just not the way most of us look. So it can give people unrealistic expectations of what a partner's body will look like.

- It can be addictive. Once people start looking at porn they can find it hard to stop.

> *There's more to sex than mere skin on skin. Sex is as much spiritual mystery as physical fact. As written in Scripture, "The two become one." Since we want to become spiritually one with the Master, we must not pursue the kind of sex that avoids commitment and intimacy, leaving us more lonely than ever – the kind of sex that can never "become one".*
>
> 1 Corinthians 6:16–17 (THE MESSAGE)

IT'S LATE!

89

- Some porn is violent and abusive.

- God designed sex to be a meaningful experience shared between a husband and wife – not something to be watched by others.

- Most porn does not address the dangers of STIs or the possibility of pregnancy and quite often contains risky sexual practices and sexual acts that a lot of people find degrading.

Porn has had a very destructive impact on many people's lives. In fact, there are many people who are seeking help from counsellors because of the negative influence that porn has had on them. Their brains have become so tuned in to the type of sex shown in porn that they have struggled to build real-life relationships.

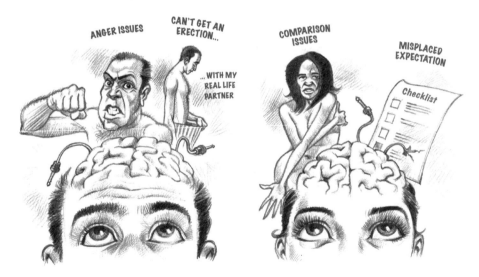

There are so many sexual images in the media and on the internet, but you can choose not to look at them. If you are ever sent a pornographic image or video clip, let a trusted adult know, and/or simply delete it. You may feel curious about it and want to look at it, but porn feeds people so many lies about sex that it's a really good idea to avoid it.

WHAT ARE YOUR VIEWS ON PORNOGRAPHY?

"People become addicted and may expect their partner to perform in that way which is unfair."

Rohan, 14

"It gives false images of what sex, relationships, and bodies are like."

Natalie, 19

"It is an issue because young people think that is what sex looks like, but it isn't."

Ethan, 14

"I don't think that much porn is created by actors/actresses who really want to be doing that kind of work, so it's bad to fund that kind of industry."

Anita, 18

"Sex is meant to be special. We shouldn't treat each other like pieces of meat."

Archie, 15

SENDING NUDE PHOTOS

Sometimes sexual images being sent around are of a person that has taken a sexual/nude photo or video of him/herself and then sent it to another person by phone or other electronic media.

What was meant as a photo for just that one person has then got into the hands of other people (accidently or deliberately) and that photo/video

is then out there for anyone to see. The government has put laws in place to protect young people, which means that it's a criminal offence for sexual photos/videos to be taken of young people who are under eighteen. So this type of image is taken very seriously, even if the young person has taken the picture or created the video themselves. Having an image like this on a phone, sending it to someone else, or posting it online are also potential criminal offences.

If you get sent a photo/video like this, don't send it on to others. Instead, report it to a trusted adult. And be wise in the photos/videos of yourself that you send or post online. If it's something you wouldn't want your parents, teachers or a future employer to see, then it's probably not a good plan to send it to others or put it on the internet. Stay safe and think before you click.

DO YOU THINK IT'S OK FOR SOMEONE TO SEND A NUDE -SELFIE TO SOMEONE ELSE?

"I think it's not ok because that picture could get sent anywhere and could even end up on pornographic sites."
Archie, 15

"*Definitely not, because it can go on to social media and be spread around everywhere.*"

Abigail, 14

"*No, because it is child pornography and it can hurt you later in life.*"

Dermot, 12

PAUSE AND PRAY

Have you ever been sent a nude photo or seen a pornographic video?

- If so, how did you feel about it? Feel free to share your thoughts with God.

- Do you think it is something you should report to an adult?

Do you know of people who have had sexual photos or videos of themselves sent around to others or posted online? You might want to ask God to help them get through it and get the right support.

Do you feel that you've been drawn to looking at porn and that it's become a bit of a habit?

- If so, be assured that you're not the only one – it's something that happens to a lot of people. But now is a good time to think it through, as watching porn is likely to start having an impact on your brain and how you relate to others.

- When you feel pulled towards it, take control: remind yourself of why it's not helpful and think of something to do instead.

- Chat to God about it and ask for his help.

- Speak to a trusted adult about it.

CHAPTER 13

ALL SORTS OF ATTRACTION

Attraction is being drawn to something because it has a quality you really like. It might be the way it looks, what it is able to do, how it tastes, what it smells like, what it sounds like or how it makes you feel.

On the journey from childhood to adulthood, young people start to experience a type of attraction called "sexual attraction". This is when someone is strongly drawn to a person because of a combination of the following things:

- the way they look (physical attraction);
- who they are – being attracted to their innermost being (personality attraction);
- the way they make you feel (emotional attraction).

When someone thinks of, or is near to, a person they like in this way, they may respond in different ways. They may feel shy, nervous or awkward, perhaps even blushing; or they might feel very excited and happy. They will probably think about that person a lot and want to spend time with them.

These types of feelings may get stronger during puberty. A young person may feel so drawn to a person they are attracted to that they feel like they want to have some kind of sexual contact with them (anything from kissing on the lips to actually having sex). So, it's different from the usual affection and love that someone feels for their friends and best mates.

While *physical* attraction can have a strong pull, the other kinds of attraction – emotional and personality attraction – are equally important. Long-term relationships such as marriage tend to be healthiest when there is a good balance of all three types of attraction between a couple.

If someone is sexually attracted to another person, they might feel like they're in love with them. In actual fact, this strong feeling may just be a "crush". It's a powerful feeling, but it might only last for a few days, weeks or months.

HAVE YOU EVER HAD A CRUSH?

"Yeah. It felt good and nervous. Also like having butterflies in your stomach when anything remotely related to that person came up in conversation."

Rohan, 14

"No, not really, but a lot of people at school do."

Joy, 12

"Yes, I have. But the bad thing is you never know if they like you until you pluck up the courage to ask."

Carlos, 11

"I'd always have a crush at school. It would vary from being excited when he gave me attention to soul-destroying when he didn't."

Natalie, 19

"I have been attracted to someone. It was a good feeling, but I was a bit nervous about talking to her."

Tyrone, 15

"Yes, but I have never told the guy! I always look forward to spending time with him."

Chloe, 14

SAME-SEX ATTRACTION

Being sexually attracted to people of the opposite sex is known as heterosexuality. This is sometimes referred to as being "straight". Some women identify themselves as being lesbian or gay because they are sexually attracted to women; and some men identify themselves as being gay because they are sexually attracted to men. Being sexually attracted to people of the same sex is called homosexuality. Some people refer to themselves as bisexual, meaning that they are sexually attracted to both men and women.

Actually, using terms such as "gay", "lesbian", "straight" or "bisexual" doesn't really reflect the fact that sexual attraction can vary over time for some people.

During puberty, young people may feel different levels and kinds of attraction to different people. Some may not be sexually attracted to anyone at this stage; others may have one special person they feel drawn to; and some may be attracted to a wide range of people.

Many young people find that they are sexually attracted to people of the same sex or both sexes. These feelings do not automatically mean that they are gay or bisexual. It may simply be that they have a crush on someone they really admire who happens to be the same sex as them. These feelings may fade. Some people who would describe themselves as heterosexual may experience same-sex attraction, just as some people who define themselves as gay may experience opposite-sex attraction during their lives. You shouldn't feel pressure to adopt a particular label like "gay" or "straight" – it's ok to take plenty of time to think about your feelings and work out who you are, not what other people think you are or should be.

WHAT CAUSES DIFFERENT ATTRACTIONS?

There has been a lot of research and debate about why not everyone is attracted to the opposite sex. Below are some of the views that different people have.

Although lots of studies have been carried out, there is not yet any conclusive evidence as to why we're attracted to particular people, and why some of us are heterosexual, some of us are gay, and some of us are bisexual. And because we are all unique individuals there may be different reasons for different people.

98

Many people who describe themselves as gay are completely comfortable with it, feeling that it's just the way they are. Others really struggle with it, feeling that it's not something their friends or family will accept, or that they don't want to be gay, or worrying that it goes against their culture or faith.

What about the Christian faith? What does the Bible say about it? Let's find out in the next chapter...

DID YOU KNOW?

Hetero is a Greek word meaning "different".

Homo is a Greek word meaning "same".

Bi is a Latin word meaning "two".

It's because they had a difficult relationship with their mother/father.

It's because of an experience they had in the past.

It's just the way I was born.

Me too, it's not something I've chosen.

CHAPTER 14

SAME-SEX ATTRACTION AND THE BIBLE

Not all Christians have the same view on this topic, because people interpret the Bible verses that mention homosexuality in different ways.

Let's take a look at three of the verses and hear some of the different views that people have:

Leviticus 18:22: *"Do not lie with a man as one lies with a woman; that is detestable."*

THE" BIBLE IS GIVING US A CLEAR WARNING THAT GOD HAS NOT CREATED US FOR THIS KIND OF ACTIVITY.

LEVITICUS GAVE IMPORTANT INSTRUCTIONS FOR HEALTHY LIVING AT THE TIME IT WAS WRITTEN, BUT IT'S NOT RELEVANT NOW.

MAYBE IT MEANS IT'S OK TO BE GAY, BUT NOT OK TO ACT ON THOSE FEELINGS AND ACTUALLY HAVE SEX WITH SOMEONE OF THE SAME SEX?

1 Corinthians 6:9–10: "Neither the sexually immoral nor idolaters nor adulterers nor male prostitutes nor homosexual offenders nor thieves nor the greedy nor drunkards nor slanderers nor swindlers will inherit the kingdom of God."

THE BIBLE IS SAYING THAT HOMOSEXUAL OFFENDERS WON'T RECEIVE GOOD THINGS FROM GOD.

I THINK THAT A "HOMOSEXUAL OFFENDER" IS SOMEONE WHO SEXUALLY ABUSES A PERSON OF THE SAME SEX. I DON'T THINK THIS IS THE SAME AS A LOVING, COMMITTED GAY RELATIONSHIP.

I THINK THIS MEANS THAT IF PEOPLE ENGAGE IN SEXUAL ACTIVITY THAT IS OUTSIDE OF GOD'S PLAN, THEY MIGHT STRUGGLE TO HAVE ACCESS TO ALL THE GOOD THINGS GOD HAS FOR THEM.

Romans 1:26–27: "Because of this, God gave them over to shameful lusts. Even their women exchanged natural relations for unnatural ones. In the same way the men also abandoned natural relations with women and were inflamed with lust for one another. Men committed indecent acts with other men, and received in themselves the due penalty for their perversion."

Wow, what a lot of differences in opinion! So, where does that leave us? What conclusions can we come to?

In actual fact, rather than focusing on a few verses in isolation, we need to think about what key messages the Bible reveals to us as a whole. What does the Bible tell us about the bigger picture of sexual union?

IN THE BEGINNING...

Genesis 2 tells us that when God created the first man, Adam, he knew that he needed a suitable companion. God took part of Adam's body (a rib) and used it to create Eve, the first woman. There were some key similarities in the man's and woman's designs but some key differences too, so that their bodies could fit together in a unique way as "one flesh".

After describing the way that God made woman, Genesis 2:24 (NIV) says, "That is why a man leaves his father and mother and is united to his wife, and they become one flesh." It's as if there is something very special about a man and his wife being united sexually, as it brings together the male and female differences together to become one.

A VERY IMPORTANT MESSAGE

Jesus and Paul both refer to Genesis 2:24 in their teachings. Have a look at the following verses: Matthew 19:4–6, Mark 10:6–9, and Ephesians 5:31.

MARRIAGE, JESUS, AND THE CHURCH

Throughout the Bible, there's quite a lot of talk about weddings and marriage. For example, sexual union between a bride and groom is celebrated in the book of Song of Songs, and the apostle Paul encourages husbands and wives to be a model of Jesus' relationship with the church, both giving all that they are and have to each other.

The Bible always describes marriage as being between a man and a woman, and sex as being designed for marriage. This indicates that sexual activity outside of a marriage between a man and a woman is not God's intention for us, no matter who we are attracted to. This is why many gay Christians decide to be celibate (not have sex).

Choosing not to have sex because we are not married or don't want to marry someone of the opposite sex is a real act of obedience to God. Making this choice is not easy and it can be challenging at times, but people can and do live fulfilling and wonderful lives without having sex.

The Bible doesn't say it's wrong to be sexually attracted to people of the same sex. It is how a person deals with the temptation to act upon these feelings that is important. Every single one of us is tempted to think and act in ways that are outside of God's plan, but God has promised to help us overcome the temptation when this happens.

LOVING GOD AND LOVING EACH OTHER

Not everyone will agree with the conclusions that have been made in this chapter. Over time you need to come to your own conclusions based on your own study of the Bible.

Jesus said (in Matthew 22:36–40, NIV) that the two greatest commandments are:

1. "Love the Lord your God with all your heart and with all your soul and with all your mind."

2. "Love your neighbour as yourself."

Loving God with your mind includes taking time to really think about what the Bible says and asking God to help you understand it. Loving your neighbour includes treating others as you would like to be treated – showing love and respect to everyone, even when we disagree with each other.

HOMOPHOBIC BULLYING

Sometimes gay and bisexual people are called horrible names or even physically attacked. This abusive behaviour is described as homophobic bullying. Some heterosexual people also experience bullying of this kind, often for no reason at all, or simply because they don't fit in with what people assume a man or a woman should be like. These types of assumptions are unhelpful, as we are all unique individuals and we like different things. For example, many boys enjoy ballet and many girls love football – both of which are great, of course, and don't have anything to do with who a person is attracted to.

The term "gay" is unfortunately often used to describe something that is bad or not cool. For example, "Those trainers are so gay" or "You're so gay". People that use this language might mean it as a joke, but making jokes which involve something as personal as who someone is or perceived to be attracted to is not a laughing matter.

Any kind of bullying is wrong – and this includes homophobic bullying.

GOD'S LOVE FOR ALL OF US

Whether we are attracted to people of the opposite sex, the same sex, a bit of both, or no one at all, God loves us abundantly, cares for us, and wants us to know him more. Who we are attracted to matters to God because he's interested in every part of us, but our sexuality is just one element of who we are. God is passionate about who we are as a whole – everything about us. He welcomes into his arms anyone who wants to know him. Our churches should be the same. None of us is excluded from being a Christian.

PAUSE AND PRAY

- How has this chapter made you feel? Do you agree with what's been said, or do you have a different opinion?

- Have you ever used the term "gay" to tease someone, even if it was just as a joke? Now might be the time to say sorry to God about that and make amends with the person you said it to.

- Have you struggled with this chapter because you are experiencing same-sex attraction? The most important thing to remember is that God loves you SO much, and having feelings of same-sex attraction doesn't change this at all. Ask God to help you process your feelings and talk to an adult you trust.

PART 4

OUR BODIES ARE PRECIOUS

CHAPTER 15

BODY BOUNDARIES

As hormones do their work, sending instructions for change around the body, young people may start to have a growing curiosity about each other's bodies as well as their own. This is a normal part of growing up. However, another important part of growing up is learning how to respect bodies – our own and other people's.

Being attracted to someone doesn't mean it is ok to touch their body, especially without their consent. Consent is when a person gives another person permission to do something.

In the case of sex, consent is when a person gives another person permission to engage in sexual activity with them. Consent is only truly given if it is given wholeheartedly, without being pressured by anyone and when the person is able to think clearly for themselves (i.e. not when they're drunk or under the influence of drugs). Also, everyone has the right to change their mind even after giving consent.

In the UK, the age of consent (the age at which a person is legally allowed to have sex) is sixteen, whether heterosexual, gay or bisexual. The age of consent is there to help protect young people, physically and emotionally, and there can be serious legal consequences if a person has sex with a boy or girl under the age of sixteen. If a person has sex with a boy or girl under the age of thirteen, it is automatically treated as rape (forced sex), even if the child agreed to have sex.

Check the laws in the country you're in if you live outside the UK.

The Bible doesn't talk about an age of consent. Instead it shows us that sex is something to be treasured and protected and that the best place for it is between a husband and wife rather than when we reach a certain age.

Avoiding sexual activity until marriage can be a big challenge. Not only can there be lots of pressure to have sex (from the media, friends, and other people), but you also have to manage the sexual feelings you may start to have. As you get older there may be times where you strongly feel like you want to have sex.

One question that many young people have is, "How far can you go before marriage?"

There's such a wide range of touch: hugging, holding hands, cuddles, kissing, deep kissing (using tongues), caressing each other's bodies with clothes on, caressing each other's bodies with clothes off, touching breasts, touching genitals, oral sex…

So, where do you draw the line outside of marriage? This is an area where real wisdom is needed.

What do you think it means to be wise when it comes to physical touch? Some of the questions worth thinking about are:

- How can I show I really value this person, rather than thinking about my own desires?

- How can I show this person that I recognize that they belong to God rather than to me?

- How will I feel if the person I like decides they aren't attracted to me anymore? Will I wish I had waited and got to know them better first before sharing any intimate physical touch with them?

- If I get involved in certain types of physical touch, will I be awakening feelings that are best kept for marriage?

- Could there be any health risks from particular types of physical touch?

Some people think that oral sex is "safe" because it doesn't cause pregnancy. However, oral sex is actually one way that STIs can spread, as infections can be passed directly from the genitals of a person who has an STI to the mouth of another person and vice versa. We'll talk more about STIs in chapter 23.

So, there are lots of things to consider when trying to make wise choices about physical touch because it's important to value and honour other people and ourselves, and because of the possible risks.

A good idea is to come up with some clear body boundaries. Boundaries are lines that separate what we feel is ok for us and what isn't ok for us.

Having these boundaries in place will help you to:

- avoid getting involved in sexual activity too early;

- say "no" to sex you may regret later;

- say a big "yes" to saving sex for marriage.

One example of a body boundary could be not touching another person's genitals, bottom, or a girl's breasts and making it clear that you don't want these parts of your body to be touched.

WHAT ADVICE WOULD YOU GIVE SOMEONE WHO IS FEELING PRESSURED TO ENGAGE IN SEXUAL ACTIVITY?

"Make sure that ahead of a party or date situation, you have already decided what will and won't happen and remind yourself of your decision. Don't be ashamed of your decision."

Anita, 18

"Ignore the people telling you to have sex!"

Karen, 13

"Waiting 'til you're married is respecting your body."

Chloe, 14

"What others think about you doesn't matter as much as what you think of yourself, and making a decision you may later regret is not worth it."

Harry, 19

"Most girls think that guys who are virgins are cute, which is a good thing."

Archie, 15

"You don't actually need to have sex."

Emma, 13

PAUSE AND PRAY

- Take some time now to think about your body boundaries.

- You might also like to ask God to help you make good decisions about your body now and in the future.

- You can ask God to help you have self-control. That means not doing what your body feels like, but letting wisdom step in first.

Waiting to have sex can be challenging, but God knows it is and he's always ready to listen to you and help you understand what it means to be wise.

And don't forget that it's absolutely fine not to have a girlfriend/boyfriend! There is actually real wisdom in developing your relationship skills by learning what it means to be a good friend and enjoying the friendships you have to help prepare you for possible girlfriend/boyfriend relationships in the future.

CHAPTER 16

WHEN BODY BOUNDARIES ARE CROSSED

Unfortunately, there are some people in the world who ignore body boundaries. They might touch someone inappropriately or persuade or force someone to get involved in sexual activity. This is called *sexual abuse*. Examples of sexual abuse are if a person:

- touches areas of a person's body (clothed or unclothed) that are sexual and private. This includes the penis and bottom for boys, and the vulva area (including the vagina), breasts, and bottom for girls – basically the parts of our body that our underwear usually covers;

- makes you show these parts of your body to them, even if they don't touch. This could be in person or via a webcam, photo or video;

- makes you touch these parts of their body;

- makes you look at these parts of their body, either in person or via a webcam, photo or video;

- makes you take part in or watch any type of sexual activity;

- makes you look at sexual pictures or videos of other people.

If anyone tries to do any of these things to you tell them to stop or say "NO" very clearly and quickly get away from them.

If they carry on or hurt you in any way or do something that you feel is not right, let a trusted adult know as soon as possible, even if that person says you need to keep it a secret. If you have ever been treated like this, it is NOT your fault, no matter what that person or anyone else says. A person who abuses is in the wrong, not the person who has been abused.

Sexual abuse is never ok, even if the person doing it is a family member, a friend or someone you know or love.

Lots of healthy touching happens in families such as cuddles, hugs, holding hands, and kissing to show love and affection for each other. This is a good thing and feels safe.

Sexual abuse is very different to this because it involves the private parts of the body.

Doctors and nurses or parents/carers may need to check these parts of your body for health reasons – for example, if you have any pain when urinating, itchiness, swelling or unusual discharge or if you have any other concerns with these parts of your body. This is not sexual abuse, but they should check with you that you're happy for them to take a look.

Do speak to a trusted adult if you want to talk about these issues further.

BEING ALERT TO UNHEALTHY FRIENDSHIPS OR RELATIONSHIPS

In a healthy friendship or relationship, both people should feel safe, accepted, cared for, respected, and free to be themselves. Friendships and relationships become unhealthy if either person harms or tries to control the other person through what they say or how they behave. Hopefully you don't have friendships like that, but here are some things to look out for:

If he/she:

- says things to you that make you feel bad about yourself;
- wants to know where you are all the time;
- always wants to check your messages;
- says things about you behind your back;
- always bosses you around;
- is physically aggressive;
- doesn't want you to be friends with other people.

If anyone treats you like this, try to talk to them and explain how it makes you feel. If they don't listen, it's best not to be friends or in a relationship with them anymore.

ONLINE BOUNDARIES

The internet is brilliant in so many ways, but we have to be alert to the negative stuff too. Some people befriend young people online using false identities. They may suggest meeting up, and sometimes young people have ended up getting hurt by doing this. They might even be forced into sexual activity with that person or others.

Be careful who you chat to online. If chatting with people you've never

met before or don't know very well, stick to public areas of forums and chatrooms, as moderators will be able to spot any dodgy behaviour. If you do have any private chats, don't share personal details about yourself such as photos, your school, home address, email address, and your full name.

RESPECTING OTHERS

Our body boundaries should be respected by other people and we must respect other people, taking care not to touch anyone in a way that could be crossing their body boundaries. No one should cause harm to us, just as we should cause no harm to others.

GOD, WHAT'S GOING ON?

It can be hard to understand why God doesn't just stop abuse from happening. The problem, however, is with humans rather than with God. God loves us so much that he allows us to make our own choices. Unfortunately, some people make choices that hurt others. God's heart breaks when people hurt each other. He helps to heal those who have been hurt and he helps them to forgive the person that did it. This is a process that can be difficult and take a long time, but it is possible.

God hates abuse. He is also so full of love that he does forgive people who abuse or cause harm if they come to him for forgiveness with a sincere heart. And if they are willing, he can help them to change their behaviour.

PAUSE AND PRAY

- What did you think about this chapter? Bring to God your feelings about it.

- Do you think that anyone has crossed your body boundaries? If so, ask God to help you to know whom to talk to about it. And remember, no matter what you might think or anyone else might say, it's not your fault.

- Are you concerned that any of your friendships might be unhealthy? Or that any of your friends might be in an unhealthy relationship? Ask God to give you wisdom so you know what to do.

- Do you really know the people you chat to online? Have a think about any online conversations you are in and consider whether you think they are healthy/ok or not. Is there anything more you can do to keep yourself safe online?

PART 5

HONOURING OTHERS AND HONOURING GOD

CHAPTER 17

HOW WE TREAT EACH OTHER

The Bible talks a lot about love. But what exactly is love? 1 Corinthians 13:4–8 (NIV) gives us a fantastic description:

> "Love is patient, love is kind. It does not envy, it does not boast, it is not proud. It is not rude, it is not self-seeking, it is not easily angered, it keeps no record of wrongs. Love does not delight in evil but rejoices with the truth. It always protects, always trusts, always hopes, always perseveres. Love never fails."

It's so easy to get jealous or get angry, isn't it? And you can probably think of times when you've reminded people of mistakes they'd rather forget. Yet love acts differently, showing great kindness, care, and forgiveness to all.

Love is not selfish and it can involve giving things up for others, such as your time, your comfort, your money or things you have. Ephesians 5:21 gets right to the point and says: "Honour Christ and put others first" (CEV).

Unfortunately, we are not always very good at putting God or others first. In fact, people can be really horrible to each other.

> **Matthew 7:12 (THE MESSAGE):** *"Here is a simple, rule-of-thumb guide for behaviour: Ask yourself what you want people to do for you, then grab the initiative and do it for them..."*
>
> **Ephesians 4:29 (THE MESSAGE):** *"Watch the way you talk. Let nothing foul or dirty come out of your mouth. Say only what helps, each word a gift."*

BULLYING

Bullying is one way that people show a complete lack of love and respect for each other. It can happen in different ways (verbally, physically, and emotionally), and it's always wrong. Some different types of bullying are:

- cyberbullying;
- racist bullying;
- bullying because of a person's faith;
- homophobic bullying;
- bullying because of a person's home situation;
- bullying because of the way someone looks;
- bullying because of a disability or learning difference;
- sexual bullying (which can include inappropriate touching, being called rude sexual names, and sexual rumours being spread about someone).

You might be able to think of other types of bullying too.

It can feel so distressing to be bullied. But something *can* be done about it. If it ever happens to you, here are some things that you can do:

- Tell a friend so that you can get support from them.

- Tell your parents/carers.

- Tell a teacher. There will be an anti-bullying policy at your school, so they will know exactly what to do (you can ask them what it says in the policy).

- In the case of cyberbullying, even though you might not really want to keep any messages that have been sent, it might actually be helpful

to keep a record of them for when you're ready to tell someone about what has been going on.

- Don't respond to abusive messages. If you do, it might encourage the sender to continue sending messages to you.

- Block the bully – you can block, delete, and unfriend people on social networking sites and if you have a phone, it may be able to block numbers.

- Don't share comments, photos or videos online that a person could use against you.

- There are lots of great organizations that can provide support (details are at the back of the book).

If you know someone is being bullied, even if they're not a friend of yours, do tell a trusted adult so that something can be done to stop it. And don't join in with bullying – it's such a hurtful thing to do.

WHAT'S YOUR ADVICE TO ANYONE GETTING BULLIED?

"Tell someone straight away. Your silence is the bully's strength."

Carlos, 11

"Get offline or block the bully."

David, 12

"Tell someone about it."

Lily, 12

"Tell an adult you trust and talk to God."

Joy, 12

"Save the messages and report them. Don't reply to a bully."

Dermot, 12

"What they say is not true. God made you in his own image and you are special."

Emma, 13

PAUSE AND PRAY

- Have you ever experienced bullying or are you experiencing bullying at the moment? Ask God to bring you comfort where that person's actions or words have hurt you. Ask God to give you strength and wisdom to know who to talk to and how to respond.

- Ask God to help you to forgive anyone who's bullied you. Even when people have treated us badly, Jesus encourages us to forgive them.

- Do you know someone who is being bullied at the moment? Ask God to help you to be a good friend to them.

- Have you ever treated someone unkindly or called someone names? You might have only said it as a joke, but it still could have come across as hurtful to the other person. Let God know that you are sorry and have a think about how you can make it up to that person.

- Is there any way you can show love to the people around you today? It might just be a smile or a word of encouragement, but it could really make a difference to that person.

CHAPTER 18

BEING STRONG AND COURAGEOUS

God could have designed us as robots – machines that follow instructions and do exactly what he says. However, God loves us so much that he gives us free will – the ability to make our own choices. His hope is that we will choose to love and follow him, not because he forces us too, but because we truly want to.

Lots of people choose not to follow God. It can seem a lot easier to fit in with what's expected in society rather than to be counter-cultural, follow Jesus, and challenge ourselves to be all that God has made us to be.

Three men who are really good examples of people who chose to show their commitment to God rather than follow what everyone else was doing are Shadrach, Meshach, and Abednego. You can find their story in the Bible in the book of Daniel (chapters 1–3).

They had been taken from their homes in Jerusalem to serve in King Nebuchadnezzar's palace in

Babylon. One day, King Nebuchadnezzar decided to build an image of gold. He ordered all the officials of the land, including Shadrach, Meshach, and Abednego, to come to its dedication. The officials were told that when the music started, they were to bow down and worship the image of gold. If they didn't, they would be thrown into a fiery furnace.

When the music began, Shadrach, Meshach, and Abednego refused to worship the image and stayed standing while everyone else bowed down. They told the king that they would not serve his idols and that their one true God could save them from the flames if he wanted to – and he did! They were thrown into the furnace, but the flames did not harm them. In fact, a mysterious fourth person appeared with them in the flames – God, either in the form of a person or an angel. So we can be encouraged that God stands with us, no matter how much we are tested in our lives.

It took real courage for these three young men to be different and stand up for what they believed. It even meant risking their lives. But they were strong in their faith and put God first.

A good place to start reading the Bible is the Gospels: Matthew, Mark, Luke, and John. They tell the story of Jesus and are a good way of getting to know who Jesus is.

UNDER PRESSURE

There are lots of areas in our life where we need to be strong in our faith and put God first, and sex is one them.

So, how can you stand firm like Shadrach, Meshach and, Abednego?

1. EXPLORE THE BIBLE.

Some people think that the Bible is just a book of rules and stories that are not relevant today, but actually it's a book full of wisdom and life. You will find that the more you let the words of the Bible soak into your mind and heart, the more you will be equipped to become all that God has made you to be.

2. GET HELP FROM THE HOLY SPIRIT.

When he went back to God the Father, Jesus knew that we would need some help. So after his resurrection, he sent the Holy Spirit to be our guide. You can ask the Holy Spirit for help whenever you need it. Ask him to give you strength to follow him, even if it means taking a different path to that of your friends and other people.

3. AVOID LOOKING AT SEXUAL IMAGES.

We're bombarded with sexual images from the media. These images can really draw us in and make us want to look at more. The more you feed your mind with images like this, the more your mind will want to be fed by them, so you need to put your self-control brakes on. Divert your eyes and mind to other things.

4. GET SUPPORT.

If you're struggling with anything to do with relationships and sex, find a trusted adult such as your parents or a youth leader at church who you can speak to about it. Remember that they were a young person once and would have also had questions about these things.

5. SEE SEX THROUGH GOD'S EYES.

The Bible is clear that sex within marriage between a man and woman is designed to be a very good thing. You don't need to feel guilty about being curious about it, because God designed it to be a wonderful experience. If you are committed to following God, then commit to sticking to God's plan for sex.

6. REMEMBER THAT GOD FORGIVES US WHEN WE MAKE MISTAKES.

God knows that as humans with free choice we may choose to do things that aren't healthy for us and not in line with his guidance for us. Lots of people, Christians included, have made mistakes to do with relationships and sex. Amazingly, God offers us complete love,

> *"If we confess our sins, he is faithful and just and will forgive us our sins and purify us from all unrighteousness."* 1 John 1:9 (NIV)

forgiveness, and comfort when we do things that are outside of his plans. This is what we call God's grace. It's something that we all need because we all make mistakes; however, knowing that God's grace is available to us doesn't mean it's ok to deliberately do things we know aren't right! One of the ways we can express our love to God is by choosing to follow him even when it's a challenge.

"Living in God's footsteps is amazing. Just try it."

Tyrone, 15

PAUSE AND PRAY

- How easy or difficult do you find it to stand up for what you believe about God, especially with your friends who aren't Christians? If you find it difficult, feel free to ask God for courage and to give you the right words when you need them. Even if the conversation doesn't go quite as planned, God loves our willingness to share his truth and love!

PART 6

NEW LIFE

CHAPTER 19

MAKING BABIES: HOW AN EGG AND A SPERM GET TOGETHER

We know that through sex, there is the potential for a new life to be created. But how exactly does this happen?

Well, during sex, semen is released from the tip of the penis into the woman's vagina.

Millions of sperm are released, but most of them don't get very far. Sperm that are not of a high quality or are not good swimmers get left behind in the vagina. The next potential obstacle for the sperm is the woman's cervix.

At certain times during the menstrual cycle there is a lot of thick mucus around the cervix, which makes it difficult for the sperm to pass through.

However, around the time of ovulation (when an egg is released) this mucus has thinned out, which makes it easier for the sperm to swim through and continue their mission to find the egg.

The sperm that have made it this far race through the uterus.

Some head up one Fallopian tube and others head up the other, but an egg is only likely to be in one of the Fallopian tubes so they have just a 50/50 chance of going the right way.

If the woman has ovulated within the previous twenty-four hours, the sperm will have the opportunity to find the egg straight away. If an egg is not there, but is released within a week, some of the sperm may still be hanging around because they can survive for up to seven days within a woman's body (although most live for up to three days).

The presence of an egg will be like a magnet for the sperm if they have swum in the right direction. Just a few hundred of the sperm make it this far and manage to find the egg.

This is when the race really heats up. Once these remaining sperm have reached the egg, only one of them can unite with it; this is a real challenge because they have to get through the egg's strong protective covering. The sperm all have a go at getting through but only one achieves it. Once this winning sperm has entered the egg (fertilized it), the egg has a reaction which means that no other sperm can enter it. The unsuccessful sperm simply die and are either absorbed by the woman's body or leave through her discharge.

Inside this fertilized egg cell, the genetic code from the winning sperm and the genetic code from the egg now combine to create a new unique genetic code for the new life that is being formed. The cell needs to find a safe place with enough space to grow so it slowly travels through the Fallopian tube into the uterus. There's a lot of activity going on within the fertilized egg cell, as it divides itself into more cells during the journey.

Once in the uterus, it finds a safe place in the lining to attach itself to, and at this point the woman is said to be pregnant.

HOW ARE TWINS CREATED?

There are two different types of twins:

IDENTICAL TWINS

Twins that look identical are formed when a fertilized egg splits in two. The two new cells have been made from the same sperm and egg, which means they will look like each other. But identical twins are still unique individuals. Even though they look extremely similar, when you get to know them you will find that they have different personalities, gifts, and abilities.

NON-IDENTICAL TWINS

Twins that do not look the same are formed when two eggs are released instead of one. A different sperm fertilizes each egg so the twins look different from each other.

CHAPTER 20

MAKING BABIES - FROM PREGNANCY TO THE GRAND ENTRY

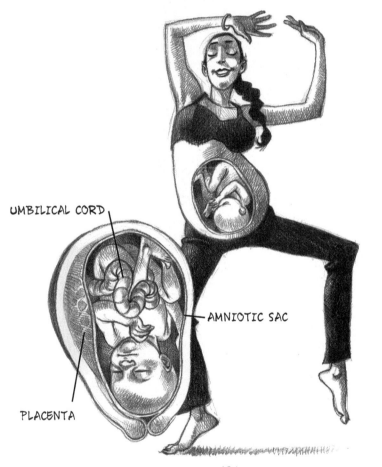

UMBILICAL CORD

AMNIOTIC SAC

PLACENTA

One sign that a female is pregnant is that she will stop having periods. This is because no new eggs are released from the ovaries during pregnancy. She can take a pregnancy test and this will confirm whether she is pregnant.

During pregnancy there are some important physical connections between the mother and developing baby. The baby is provided with nutrients and oxygen from the mother through an organ called the **placenta**. This is attached to the lining of the uterus and is connected to the baby by the **umbilical cord**. The placenta also draws away carbon dioxide and waste products, including the baby's urine.

It's not just nutrients and oxygen that the developing baby needs. It also needs to be protected as the mother moves around. Protection is provided by the sac of special fluid that it grows in, the **amniotic sac**.

As you can see, the whole process from the man's sperm entering the woman to an egg being fertilized and then developing into a baby has been really well designed and involves so much detail. After about nine months (forty weeks) the baby is ready to be born.

THE GRAND ENTRY

When the baby is ready, labour begins. Labour is the mother's body's way of preparing for birth, making a way for the baby to come out. Over the period of time it takes (which varies), there are different stages.

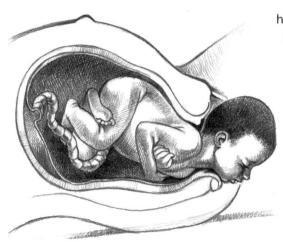

The amniotic sac that has been protecting the baby inside the uterus breaks either just before or during labour. The mother will notice water (amniotic fluid) coming out of her vagina when this happens – it's not something she can control.

The cervix needs to open up so that the baby

can get through. Muscles in the uterus help the cervix to open and then later on they help to push the baby out. The mother can feel these muscle movements over and over again and these are called "contractions".

The pushing that the muscles in the uterus do, as well as the strong pushing of the mother, helps the baby to make its way through the mother's vagina. The vagina is able to expand to enable the baby to move out.

It's a wonderful moment. It might not sound like the baby is very happy about it because it will start crying, but this is a good, healthy sign that it's fine. It's just getting used to being in a completely new environment.

After the birth, the umbilical cord connecting it to the mother is cut and the baby is left with a belly button where the cord was. The placenta is no longer needed so it comes out of the woman's body the same way as the baby did, helped by more contractions.

If doctors are concerned that there may be difficulties for either the mother or the baby during birth, they can use an alternative method to get the baby out – a Caesarean section (or C-section). She will be given an anaesthetic (so she doesn't feel anything) and the doctors will then carefully cut through her skin and remove the baby and the placenta. Afterwards, the mother's skin is stitched back together enabling the cut to heal.

Sometimes a baby is born prematurely, before nine months have passed. If this happens, the baby may need a bit of extra support at hospital before being taken home. Sometimes a baby is still in the mother's uterus after nine months, but this could cause problems as there's not enough room for it to keep growing. If the baby has not been born one or two weeks after the due date, the mother will be given advice about inducing the birth (triggering the birth process medically).

DIFFERENT WAYS THAT BABIES ARE MADE

If a couple are trying to have a baby, but don't seem to be able to, they can speak to their doctor for advice.

A sperm might not be able to fertilize an egg because:

- Either the man or the woman has other health issues.

- Eggs are not being released or are not able to move very far.

- Not enough sperm are contained in the semen (low sperm count).

- The sperm are not very strong swimmers and don't get as far as the egg.

Intrauterine (artificial) insemination is when sperm that have been supplied by the man are inserted into the woman's uterus by a doctor using a special tube. This cuts down on the journey the sperm would normally have to make and brings it closer to its goal of reaching the egg. If the man's sperm have been struggling to reach an egg, donor sperm can be used from another man.

IVF (in vitro fertilization) is when an egg that has been removed from a woman's ovaries by doctors is fertilized in a laboratory by a sperm taken from a man. The fertilized egg is then inserted into the women's uterus in the hope that it will attach itself to the uterus lining so that the woman becomes pregnant. If a woman's eggs can't be fertilized for some reason, a donor egg can be used from another woman.

With advances in technology, there are also other methods, including freezing eggs and sperm for use in the future.

JUST AS SPECIAL

Children can also be brought into a family through fostering and adoption. Some parents are not able to look after their children, but there are many people who welcome these children into their home, love and look after them, and a new family unit is formed.

WOULD YOU LIKE TO HAVE CHILDREN ONE DAY?

"I would like to have children, but when I'm around 32, not when I'm young."

Dermot, 12

"I can't wait to have children, I'm very excited! But I'm certainly not prepared or experienced enough to have one now as a teen."

Anita, 18

"I need to be financially and emotionally ready to have a child before I do, which I could never be as a teenager."

Harry, 19

"I don't want to have a child ever!"

Lily, 12

"I would love to have children after I am married. I like the idea of having my own family. I would not be able to have a kid as a teenager. I have way better things to do."

Archie, 15

CHAPTER 21

NOT MAKING BABIES: WHAT IS CONTRACEPTION?

Babies bring joy to their families and can be a huge amount of fun. However, it takes lots of hard work to look after them. Their nappies need changing,

they need feeding regularly, they cry, they scream – even in the middle of the night. Then of course there's the expense to think about. Bringing up a child costs a lot of money.

So it's good to be as ready as possible to look after a baby before having one.

If a couple decide they are not ready, or perhaps they have already had the number of children they want, they may decide that they would like to have sex without the possibility of pregnancy. They may choose to use contraception (a device which prevents pregnancy).

A number of options are available. Most of them are designed for women, not men. However, it is good for a man and woman to talk about contraception together, as deciding whether to have a baby or not should be an equal responsibility.

For a woman to become pregnant, the following things need to happen:

1. An egg needs to be released from one of the woman's ovaries.

2. One sperm (out of millions) needs to reach the egg.

3. The fertilized egg needs to travel to the uterus and find a secure place to attach itself to so that it can grow safely.

Contraception stops one or more of these things from happening.

CONTRACEPTION THAT RELEASES HORMONES

Some contraceptives work by releasing hormones into the female's body. The effect of these hormones can be one or more of the following:

- to stop ovaries from releasing eggs;

- to cause the natural mucus around the cervix to get thicker, making it much more difficult for sperm to pass through the cervix;

- to prevent the lining of the uterus from thickening so that a fertilized egg can't implant itself.

Contraceptives that release hormones include:

- the pill: there are different types of pill. The instructions for each type need to be followed carefully.

- the contraceptive injection: lasts for eight to twelve weeks depending on the type of injection.

- the contraceptive implant: a device that is inserted into a female's upper arm and lasts for up to three years.

Other hormonal contraceptive methods include:

- the patch;

- the vaginal ring;

- the IUS (intrauterine system).

The diaphragm and the cap are other barriers – they stop sperm getting through the cervix. They are used with spermicide, a gel that kills sperm.

Sperm can also be destroyed by the action of the IUD (intrauterine device). It's not a barrier method – it's a small device containing copper that is inserted into the woman's uterus. The copper alters the surrounding fluids and this reaction stops sperm from surviving.

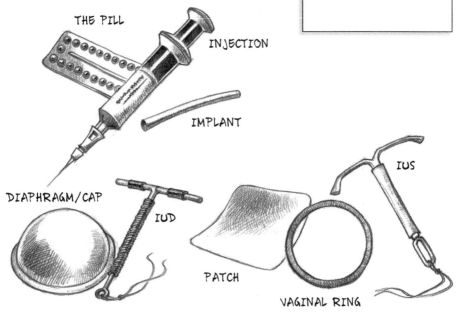

THE PILL

INJECTION

IMPLANT

IUS

DIAPHRAGM/CAP

IUD

PATCH

VAGINAL RING

CONTRACEPTION THAT ACTS AS A BARRIER

Sperm have the potential to be excellent swimmers; however, they can be stopped if there is a reliable barrier in place.

The most common barrier used is the male condom. When used correctly, it keeps sperm within the condom and doesn't allow them to swim through. Male condoms are made from thin latex (rubber) or a flexible material called polyurethane, and they fit over an erect penis. Female condoms are also available and are carefully placed inside the vagina, but male condoms are more commonly used. Condoms are the only form of contraception that can also protect against many sexually transmitted infections (STIs).

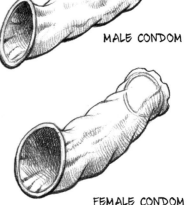

MALE CONDOM

FEMALE CONDOM

OTHER TYPES OF CONTRACEPTION

If a couple are certain that they don't want to have children or any more children, either the man or the woman can have an operation called sterilization – a procedure in which essential tubes involved in conception are blocked off (fallopian tubes in women and the vas deferens in men).

Some people prefer a completely **natural** approach. Natural family planning is where a couple avoid sex when a woman is most likely to get pregnant – that is, around the time when an egg has been released. Women obviously don't have a window into their ovaries so that they can see whether an egg has been released or not, and sometimes the menstrual cycle is not regular, so a lot of thought, care, and understanding of the body need to go into this method.

All of the different types of contraception have advantages and disadvantages, and a couple will need to talk with a doctor or nurse to decide the best type for them.

MYTH BUSTERS

MYTH *A woman won't get pregnant if she has sex in certain positions or if she has sex standing up or in water.*

TRUTH *If a couple are not using contraception, the woman can get pregnant no matter what position they have sex in or where they do it.*

MYTH *A woman can avoid getting pregnant by jumping up and down or washing herself after sex.*

TRUTH *Jumping up and down or washing does not stop sperm from reaching an egg.*

MYTH *A woman can't get pregnant if she has sex during her period.*

TRUTH *In some cases, sperm can hang around in a woman's body for up to seven days. If for any reason the woman releases a new egg much earlier than usual, while sperm are still in her body, pregnancy can occur. This is not common, but it can happen.*

CHAPTER 22

A BIG QUESTION: WHEN DOES LIFE BEGIN?

From the moment a sperm fertilizes an egg until the time a baby is born, there's a whole lot of development going on.

STAGE 1: FERTILIZATION

This is the moment when a sperm unites with an egg. The fertilized egg is known as a zygote. It contains key information such as whether the cell will develop into a boy or a girl, eye colour, and adult height.

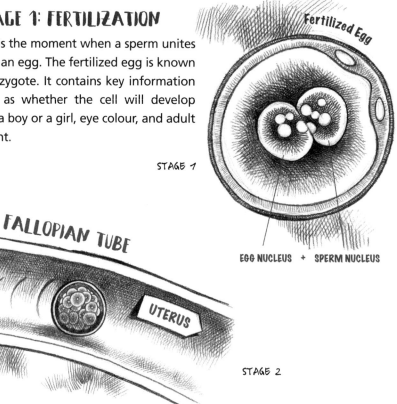

Fertilized Egg

STAGE 1

EGG NUCLEUS + SPERM NUCLEUS

FALLOPIAN TUBE

UTERUS

STAGE 2

STAGE 2: TRAVELLING TO THE UTERUS

The zygote travels into the uterus where there is room to grow. As it travels, it starts dividing so that it becomes a ball of small cells.

STAGE 3: IMPLANTATION

This developing ball of cells, which is now called a blastocyst, attaches itself to the lining of the uterus. The outside part of the blastocyst becomes the placenta; the inside part is called the embryo and this continues to develop.

FALLOPIAN TUBE

THICKENED UTERUS LINING

STAGE 3

STAGE 4: DEVELOPMENT

STAGE 4

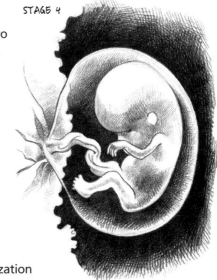

After about eight weeks, the embryo has developed dramatically and is now called a fetus. Most of the major structures and tissues of a human body are in place, including the heart. The fetus continues to grow and develop until birth.

In the previous chapter we talked about contraception.

- Some types of contraception prevent sperm from fertilizing an egg.

- Other types can work after fertilization by preventing implantation. This means that the blastocyst disintegrates because it is unable to grow.

If a couple have decided to use contraception, a big part of their decision about which type to use will depend on when they believe life begins.

Many people think that life begins at fertilization, when the first cell of a new human being is created. These people may choose not to use contraception that can work after this stage.

Others think that life doesn't start until implantation, when the blastocyst is directly attached to its mother and can receive nutrients and oxygen.

Some people don't recognize the growing baby as a person until even later stages, such as when its heart starts beating, or when it has developed enough to be able to survive outside its mother's body, or when it is born.

ABORTION

These issues are often discussed in debates about abortion. Abortion is a medical procedure carried out to end a pregnancy. Laws about abortion vary depending on the country or state within a country. In Great Britain (England, Scotland, and Wales) a woman can have an abortion up to twenty-four weeks of pregnancy if two doctors agree.

People respond to abortion in different ways. Some feel very angry or sad because the potential for life is being taken away from the unborn baby. Others may feel that the woman or couple have good reasons for not wanting the developing baby to be born. Perhaps the woman was raped (forced to have sex), or the woman doesn't feel emotionally or mentally able to go through with the pregnancy. Some couples choose to go through with an abortion if scans show that the baby will be born with severe disabilities. There may be very serious cases where an abortion is carried out if pregnancy is putting the mother's life in danger.

HOW DOES GOD FEEL ABOUT ABORTION?

In Psalm 139:13–16, David writes:

"For you created my inmost being; you knit me together in my mother's womb. I praise you because I am fearfully and wonderfully made; your works are wonderful, I know that full well. My frame was not hidden from you when I was made in the secret place. When

I was woven together in the depths of the earth, your eyes saw my unformed body." (NIV)

In God's eyes, we were special beings even from our very beginning. In Jeremiah 1:5, God says, "Before I formed you in the womb I knew you, before you were born I set you apart" (NIV). Even before the fertilized cell reached the uterus (the womb) God knew us and saw us as precious. Abortion, then, must be something that saddens God.

Yet no one should look down on a woman who has had an abortion or the man who has made that decision with her. Jesus says, "Do not judge, or you too will be judged" (Matthew 7:1 NIV).

We all do things in our lives that sadden God. However, when we talk to him about it and let him know that we are sorry, he forgives us abundantly and helps us to move forward.

Women who are facing an unplanned pregnancy can get advice from trained counsellors who can help them think about all the options

available to them: keeping the baby, adoption, and abortion. It is very important that when talking about abortion the counsellor explains the procedure and the possible emotional consequences the woman may face afterwards, sometimes years later. Some women may have regrets or experience feelings of great loss or guilt.

The Bible urges us to show love and compassion to people. We might not agree with abortion, but we must not judge those who have made that choice. Instead, there may be ways we can support and help them if they need it.

WHAT ARE YOUR FEELINGS ABOUT ABORTION?

"The choice should be left to the person in question. I don't think if it was my child I would advocate it, especially as there are other options such as adoption. However, the choice should still be there."

Tyrone, 15

"I think it is wrong because even if you don't want to be a mum, you should still let a baby live."

Lily, 12

"I don't think it's right. I just can't see how people don't believe the organism inside a woman is not a baby."

Anita, 18

"I think it is very sad but wouldn't judge someone who made that decision."

Harry, 19

PAUSE AND PRAY

- What do you think about these last few chapters? What do you think about the whole reproduction process?

- When do you think life begins?

- You might like to spend some time re-reading Psalm 139:13–16 and Jeremiah 1:5, remembering that God has known and loved you even before you were fully formed. And, if you like, spend some time now chatting to God about how these verses make you feel.

PART 7

HANDLE WITH CARE

CHAPTER 23

SEXUALLY TRANSMITTED INFECTIONS

One of the many reasons why it is important for people to think carefully about sex is because there are infections that can be passed from one person to another through sexual activity (including vaginal sex, oral sex, and anal sex) and close genital skin contact.

Learning about these sexually transmitted infections (STIs) helps us to stay safe and to understand how God's plan for sex is designed to protect our health as well as our hearts.

There are a number of different STIs, but the ones we will focus on in this chapter are chlamydia, gonorrhoea, syphilis, genital warts, and genital herpes.

STIS CAUSED BY BACTERIA

Chlamydia, gonorrhoea, and syphilis are all bacterial infections.

A person who has been infected with chlamydia or gonorrhoea may not be aware it is there because it can hide in the body unnoticed. Unfortunately, these infections can cause damage inside a person's reproductive system without them knowing, and this can affect their fertility (ability to have children).

Syphilis is more obvious. It causes a sore at the point of infection and then other symptoms, such as a rash and flu-like illness. If it is not treated it can go on to cause serious health problems.

Chlamydia, gonorrhoea, and syphilis can all be identified easily by tests and because they are bacterial, they can be cured by taking prescribed antibiotics.

STIS CAUSED BY VIRUSES

Genital herpes and genital warts are caused by viruses. Treatment is available to reduce the symptoms, but there is no cure and they can reoccur.

Genital herpes can cause blistery sores in the genital area or anus. A person might also have pain when urinating and experience flu-like symptoms. Genital warts are small growths that appear in the genital area and anus.

Many people don't get any obvious symptoms with genital herpes or genital warts and might not know they have them, but may still be able to pass them on. As well as being passed through sexual activity, genital herpes and genital warts can also be spread by close genital skin contact.

Genital warts are caused by certain strains of a virus called HPV (human papilloma virus). There are other types of HPV that can lead to cervical cancer and other cancers. In the UK, girls aged between twelve and thirteen are offered a vaccine to help protect against cervical cancer and genital warts.

HIV is also a virus and we'll explore this in the next chapter.

TESTING

You can't tell by looking at someone whether they have an STI or not.

A person who has an STI may not even know it is there. So, if a person has had unprotected sex, they should get tested, even if they don't have any symptoms. Some couples make the wise decision to get tested before they get married if either one or both of them has had sex. Testing can be done at sexual health clinics and is very straightforward, involving a urine test or blood test or analysing cells taken from the vagina or penis. If a test is positive the doctor or nurse can provide suitable treatment and advice.

SIGNS/SYMPTOMS OF AN STI

Some STIs are not noticeable. In other cases there may be symptoms such as:

- pain when urinating;

- sores, blisters, lumps or rashes around the genitals or anus;

- unusual discharge from the vagina or penis.

OTHER REASONS FOR THESE SYMPTOMS

Many people get these symptoms for reasons other than sex. For example, thrush is a fungal infection that can cause itching, an unusual discharge, and pain when urinating. It is very common in girls, and can occur in boys too. Although it is possible for it to be passed on through sexual activity it is more likely to be caused by other factors, including hormonal changes, chemical changes in the vagina, and using perfumed products around the genital area.

Many women experience change in their usual discharge that is caused by an infection called **bacterial vaginosis**. Like thrush, it is not classed as an STI. It is caused by bacterial changes in the vagina and using perfumed products around the vagina.

Pain when urinating can be a symptom of a urinary tract infection. A doctor or nurse can help to identify the problem and provide the necessary treatment.

CONDOMS

Condoms provide a barrier between two people having sex – stopping the sexual fluid of each person getting into the body of the other person.

Condoms are very effective at preventing the spread of many STIs (including chlamydia, gonorrhoea, syphilis, and HIV), if they are:

- **not damaged;**
- **not past the expiry date;**
- **made to the right standard;**
- **used correctly every time.**

For STIs that are spread by close genital skin contact, condoms will only be effective if they fully cover the affected area. Genital warts and genital herpes, for example, might be on a part of the genital area not covered by the condom.

Condoms offer very good protection against many STIs and make sex much safer, but they do have limitations and they cannot offer a 100 per cent guarantee. The most effective ways a person can protect themselves are to not engage in sexual activity or to stay faithful to a partner who is uninfected.

CHAPTER 24

HIV AND AIDS

HIV AND AIDS

HIV stands for *H*uman *I*mmunodeficiency *V*irus. This means that it is a virus that is passed between humans, and it causes the immune system to stop working properly.

AIDS stands for *A*cquired *I*mmune *D*eficiency *S*yndrome. "Acquired" means getting something from a specific action. HIV can weaken the immune system so much that it is unable to fight germs and infections. The word "syndrome" means that the body will start showing lots of different signs and symptoms (such as rashes, sores, and body pains) according to the different illnesses the body is experiencing.

Our bodies are equipped with a very important feature – the immune system. It fights against infections, viruses, and harmful bacteria.

Of all the STIs, HIV is the most serious because it attacks the immune system, putting a person at risk of getting seriously ill.

HIV targets CD4 cells, fighter cells within the immune system. When an HIV particle attaches itself to a CD4 cell, it is able to reprogram it – telling it to produce more HIV particles instead of killing them. So the CD4 cell becomes an HIV factory. The CD4 cell ends up dying and leaves more HIV particles in its place. These are able to continue their mission and find other CD4 cells to reprogram and destroy. So the number of CD4 cells goes down and the number of HIV particles goes up, weakening the immune system.

This process can take a long time, and, unless a person gets tested, they may not realize they have been infected until years later when symptoms start to appear.

If nothing is done, the immune system will get so weak that serious illnesses will take hold of the body. At this point, a person living with HIV is said to have AIDS. A person does not die of AIDS though; it is simply the last stage of HIV. They may die of one of the illnesses that the immune system is not successful in defeating. Sadly, millions of people around the world have already died because they reached this last stage of HIV, AIDS.

GOOD NEWS

Things have changed dramatically though and in many countries today, especially in developed countries, most people who are HIV positive don't reach this last stage of HIV. This is because although there is not yet a cure, improvements in medicine (ARVs or antiretrovirals) mean that the action of the HIV virus can be slowed down significantly. This means that people living with HIV can have a normal or near-normal life expectancy if they have been diagnosed early enough. However, not everyone who is HIV positive is able to access ARVs, especially in poorer areas of the world, so there is still work to be done to make sure that everyone who needs ARVs gets them.

Even though HIV can be managed through taking medicine, it's important to note that ARVs can have strong side effects, the instructions have to be followed very carefully, and every effort needs to be made by the person who is HIV positive to stay as healthy as possible. Living with HIV can also have a big impact in other areas of life, such as relationships. It is still a serious virus so we need to make sure we know how to prevent the spread of HIV and how to support those living with it.

HOW IS HIV TRANSMITTED?

Five bodily fluids are able to transmit HIV from an HIV positive person to another person. These are:

- semen;
- vaginal fluid;
- rectal secretions (mucus/moisture in the rectum, which is the passage just above the anus – transmission through rectal secretions can happen during anal sex);

- blood;
- breast milk.

So, the three ways that HIV can be transmitted are:

1. unprotected sex (sex without a condom) with a person who is HIV positive;

2. blood from a person who is HIV positive getting into the bloodstream of another person – this can happen to drug users if they share needles for injecting drugs;

3. an HIV positive pregnant woman passing HIV to her baby during pregnancy, birth, and breast feeding. However, the risk of this happening can be greatly reduced if the mother:
   - takes ARVs;
   - feeds the baby on an alternative to breast milk;
   - has a Caesarean section delivery if the doctors recommend it.

Ways that people can protect themselves from getting HIV through sexual contact include:

- not engaging in sexual activity;
- being faithful to one uninfected partner;
- using a condom correctly.

It is important that anyone who has had unprotected sex with someone whose HIV status is unknown gets tested as you can't tell by looking at someone if they have HIV. If a couple get married or choose to have sex before marriage and one of them is HIV positive, they can get advice from an HIV clinic and use condoms to help protect the HIV-negative person.

You can't get HIV from:

- kissing, hugging, holding hands or spending time with a person who is HIV positive;
- sharing food and drink or living in the same house as someone who is HIV positive;

- toilet seats, swimming pools, mosquito bites, dog bites, coughs and sneezes;

- getting injections from a nurse or doctor – clean needles are always used;

- donating blood;

- receiving a blood transfusion in the UK (donated blood is screened carefully);

- getting a body piercing or tattoo from a registered/licensed store (where they have to use clean, sterile needles).

SHOWING LOVE

Those living with HIV have sometimes been treated in a negative way by some people. This is wrong – Jesus teaches us to love and care for people, and not to mistreat anyone. In John 13:34 (NIV), Jesus says, "A new command I give you: Love one another. As I have loved you, so you must love one another."

CHAPTER 25

THE HUMAN BODY: HANDLE WITH CARE

Throughout this book, we have seen how amazing the human body is and some of the things it is capable of. In chapter 5 we looked at keeping ourselves clean. Other ways that we can look after our bodies are exercising regularly, drinking plenty of water, eating a balanced, healthy diet, avoiding putting unhealthy substances into our bodies, and getting enough rest and sleep.

EXERCISE

Exercise benefits us in so many ways:

- It strengthens our heart, which is really important because it is responsible for delivering oxygen to all parts of our body (through blood).
- It helps to strengthen our muscles.
- It gives us more energy and makes us feel good.
- It helps us to get rid of stress.
- It helps us to be flexible and have greater movement in our bodies.

According to experts, you should exercise for at least thirty minutes every day. This can include brisk walking, so it's not as hard as it might sound! At least twice a week you should do some exercise that really gets the heart pumping, so that your heart gets a good workout and stays strong and healthy. This could include running, gymnastics, cycling, swimming, football, netball, rugby, hockey, tennis, basketball, aerobics, dancing or athletics – basically anything that is really active.

WATER

Did you know that more than half of a healthy body is made up of water? Water is an essential ingredient in our bodies as it has lots of important roles to play. It is in our blood, it is a vital part of our digestive system, and it enables waste to come out of our body. We each need different amounts of water depending on the size of our body, but make sure you drink plenty and limit fizzy drinks and squash, which are very sugary and can cause damage to your teeth.

FOOD

Eating a balanced, healthy diet doesn't mean going on a diet where you don't eat much. It means eating regular meals (including breakfast) and choosing a variety of foods from the basic food groups. People with allergies or intolerances have to avoid certain foods and replace them with other types of food, but in general we should eat:

- a good, healthy amount of **starchy carbohydrates** – examples include bread, rice, pasta, potatoes, and cereals;

- at least five portions of **fruit and vegetables** every day;

- some **protein** – such as meat, fish, eggs, nuts, beans, and lentils;

- some **milk and dairy products**;

- just a small amount of **food and drinks high in fat and/or sugar**. These are often really tasty, but should be limited as much as possible, as too much of these will work against our health rather than for it.

People, young and old, can feel pressure to lose weight, gain weight or make other changes to try to be more like the images they see around them in the media. Some people even go as far as having plastic surgery, which can sometimes go wrong and cause damage to the body. It's important for us to remember that we are all designed to be different and unique, not to look the same. Our body shapes are different and that is a good thing. There are people who are naturally big, people who are naturally small, and lots of different shapes and sizes in between. Exercising regularly and eating healthily will help us to maintain the right body shape for us and help to keep our body functioning well.

There can be times in people's lives when they struggle with food, either because they rely on it too much to give them comfort when they are feeling down, or because they become convinced they are overweight when actually they are not. If food makes you feel uncomfortable in any way then speak to your parents or another trusted adult about it.

SMOKING, ALCOHOL, AND DRUGS

Another way of keeping our bodies in good condition is by avoiding smoking, alcohol, and drug-taking. These things can give people a temporary high or temporary feeling of relaxation, but they can cause damage to the body, especially when used regularly or in large amounts, and can lead to serious health conditions. It's important that we really think about what chemicals and substances we are putting into our bodies, how they will affect our ability to make healthy choices, and how they will impact our health in the future.

REST AND SLEEP

Our mind and body need a chance to build up energy again after using up so much during the day. Rest can be simply taking a break from whatever you are doing and spending time doing something else. It can include doing exercise to take a break from studying, or it could be reading a book, playing a game, watching TV or taking a complete break by sleeping. Eleven- to fourteen-year-olds tend to need around ten hours' sleep each night, but this can vary. It can be tempting to spend a lot of time in front of electronic screens when you're resting, but make sure you don't stay in front of any type of screen for too long as your eyes will also need to rest.

PAUSE AND PRAY

- How well are you looking after your body at the moment? Is there anything you could be doing to care for yourself a bit more?

- What will you do to protect yourself from getting STIs?

- Millions of people across the world are living with HIV. You may like to pray for them now that they will get the access to ARV medication that they need and that people would not discriminate against those living with HIV.

- Feel free to chat to God now about any concerns you have about your body and how to look after yourself well.

FINAL WORDS

We've seen throughout this book that puberty is jam packed with hormone activity, triggering new feelings and changes in the body. With all that's going on it's good to remember that God is with us, always pouring out love for us and cheering us on through life.

Even when we make mistakes, he loves us. Even when we have angry or negative or weird thoughts, he loves us. Nothing can separate us from God's love.

We can choose to respond to God by loving him back! We can do that by telling him we love him, giving thanks to him, showing love to other people, spending time chatting/praying/listening to him, taking time to see him in creation, reading the Bible, and sticking to what the Bible says – being obedient.

DO YOU LIKE PRAYING?

"I like praying because I can talk to God about anything, and he listens."

David, 12

"I can let my thoughts out when I pray."

Joy, 12

171

"Sometimes praying feels like a chore but other times it can be useful."

Ethan, 14

"I don't like praying aloud, but it's nice to feel like someone is always listening when I do pray internally."

Natalie, 19

"I love praying as I get time with God, my best friend, and I can do it whenever I want wherever I want."

Dermot, 12

"I like praying, because I can tell God about all my feelings."

Lily, 12

It can be really helpful to talk about what's going on in your life (the ups and the downs) with other Christians – perhaps members of your family, friends, church community or youth group, if you are part of one.

Even though you are young, God can use you to be a great help to others. 1 Timothy 4:12 says: "Don't let anyone make fun of you, just because you are young. Set an example for other followers by what you say and do, as well as by your love, faith, and purity" (CEV).

You can be an example to those who don't yet understand what Christianity is all about. Help them to see that it's not a religion full of rules and regulations, but that it's all about living life to the full.

Never forget how valuable and loved by God you are.

HOW WOULD YOU DESCRIBE GOD?

"God is great, loving and he cares for us a lot."

David, 12

"He is awesome!! Indescribable! I love him!"

Karen, 13

"The person who created me and has a plan for me and loves me for who I am and is my best friend who I can always trust."

Dermot, 12

"Beyond words."

Joy, 12

"He is very current, and not a mystical man in history books."

Harry, 19

"God is a loving father who designed and created you and loves you unconditionally. There is nothing you can do for him to love you less. He is completely forgiving and is just waiting for you to come to him."

Natalie, 19

A CLOSING PRAYER

Here's a prayer you can pray if you'd like to:

> *Dear God, thank you for my life and all the good things in it. I pray that you would help me as I make the journey from childhood to adulthood. Help me to get used to the changes that are taking place in my body and the new feelings I will experience. Help me feel calm if angry thoughts rise up in me. Help me feel peace when I feel stressed or confused. Help me to see myself the way you see me and help me to recognize the gifts, abilities, and skills you have placed in me.*
>
> *Thank you Jesus that you love me so much that you died for me, which means that I'm forgiven for everything I've done wrong. Thank you that you rose from the dead, that you're alive and real.*
>
> *Help me to make good choices now and in the future and help me to follow you with all my heart, mind, and strength.*
> *Amen!*

FURTHER SUPPORT

For further advice and help (in the UK), you can contact the following organizations.

ChildLine: www.childline.org.uk

You can contact ChildLine about anything you're concerned about. You can: speak to a counsellor on 0800 1111 anytime (it's confidential, free, and won't appear on the phone bill);
speak to a counsellor by going to the "get support" area of the website. You can contact them through 1-2-1 chat online (like instant messenger) or by email.

CEOP (Child Exploitation and Online Protection Centre): www.thinkuknow.co.uk

CEOP provide information, advice, and help if you are concerned about anything to do with online activity.

selfharmUK: www.selfharm.co.uk

selfharmUK is a project dedicated to supporting young people impacted by self-harm, providing a safe space to talk and ask questions.

beat: www.b-eat.co.uk

Beat is a charity supporting anyone affected by eating disorders or difficulties with food, weight, and shape.

ACKNOWLEDGMENTS

This book would not have come into being without the support of many wonderful people who have cheered me on, prayed for me, and given me advice and a listening ear along the way.

Thank you so much to family, friends, and colleagues who read drafts of the book and gave such helpful feedback, and challenged me where it was needed. Thanks also to friends and colleagues who supported me in organising focus groups – I really appreciate the time and thought you put into this.

Huge thanks to my Mum and Dad for their love and support and for championing me in all I do.

Alex Webb-Peploe, thank you so much for doing such a fantastic job with the illustrations, for bringing the book to life, and for your patience with me!

Thanks to the Sir Halley Stewart Trust, Urban Saints, the Well of Hope, and generous family and friends for enabling the book to be illustrated.

And most of all, thank you to all the young people who contributed to the production of this book, including the content, choice of illustrator and the title. Special thanks go to all the young people who took part in the conversations that are in the book – I'm so grateful for your input and your willingness to share your thoughts and insights about these topics so openly. You are all truly amazing.

The views expressed within this book are those of the author and not necessarily those of the Sir Halley Stewart Trust.